Pick-up Stix

Pick-up Stix

Jacqueline Lorraine Conwell

authorHOUSE®

AuthorHouse™ LLC
1663 Liberty Drive
Bloomington, IN 47403
www.authorhouse.com
Phone: 1-800-839-8640

Published by AuthorHouse   06/06/2013

ISBN: 978-1-4817-5988-5 (sc)
ISBN: 978-1-4817-5987-8 (hc)
ISBN: 978-1-4817-5986-1 (e)

Library of Congress Control Number: 2013910157

Any people depicted in stock imagery provided by Thinkstock are models, and such images are being used for illustrative purposes only.
Certain stock imagery © Thinkstock.

This book is printed on acid-free paper.

I write differently from what I speak, I speak differently from what I think, I think differently from the way I ought to think, and so it all proceeds into the deepest darkness.
—Franz Kafka, *Letters to Ottla and the Family*

To my parents, Jack and Doreen, for instilling in me that "can't" is *not* a word.

—Prologue—

I'm happy that the friendship between Alexia and me is on the mend. The fact that she was almost taken away from all of us unexpectedly makes my skin crawl to this day. I try to keep the memory locked away, but whenever I look at her, I can't help but remember what happened. I was so afraid that I'd never get to speak to her again, especially since it would have meant that I wouldn't have been able to apologize to her after the huge argument we had on campus . . .

When she stormed away from both Jordan and me that day with our childhood friends, Matt and Samantha, following close behind her to the parking lot, I had no idea that I'd get a call about her being in a horrible accident about thirty minutes later. I got to the scene as quickly as I could, but by the time I arrived, she was already being sped off to the hospital. I visited her every day along with her parents during the winter break, and I made it a point to visit her after my last class of the day when the spring semester started. Occasionally, I ran into Matt and Samantha when I visited; Jordan never came with me. Because of what he calls my "misplaced loyalty," I've been subjected to running ridiculous errands to try to make up for quality time we've lost. I hate it.

I'm still not happy with where I am in regard to this so-called relationship. And I don't think that'll change. After I admitted that to myself about a year into it, I started coming to the beach to bury letters and lists in the sand. This isn't even the type of thing I usually write when I come here. I usually jot down some of the qualities that'd be nice to find in the perfect significant other. Julian, a guy who has grown pretty fond of Alexia ever since he moved to town, brought what Jordan was missing to my attention. I'm not sure what he is to Alexia, but there's no mistaking that there's a strong sense of loyalty between them, among other things. After seeing that firsthand in the recovery room when she woke up, I realized that there were quite a few qualities that Jordan obviously lacked.

What I'm writing probably belongs in a private journal or something. Part of me wants someone to find what I've been burying, while the other part of me is embarrassed because I feel like what I'm doing is silly. The idea that somehow, someway, any of what I write about a perfect anything *could possibly come to fruition is the silly part about all of this. I've convinced myself that this'll help me hang on to whatever hope that's left that there's something—or someone—better out there for me. That's the only thing that's been keeping me going:* hope.

I feel like I've wasted a beach day since I wrote off topic today. I have to remember to try and stay focused the next time. It's okay to take a break from the usual type of composition though, right?

If anyone out there is listening or has read any of these, thanks for not thinking I'm crazy.

—Alora

—Chapter 1—

Tomorrow I'll get back on track. No more of this journal format gibberish, I thought to myself.

After gently tearing out the now full sheet of paper from the notebook I was writing in, I placed it, and the pen I was writing with, beside me. Slowly, I began to dig a hole in the warm sand as I read over what I'd just written. Without warning, a strong breeze snatched the paper out of my hands. I quickly jumped up and grabbed it out of the air before it got away from me, landing softly back in the sand next to the hole I had dug.

"That was close."

Folding the paper into a neat square, I dropped it into the hole and slowly pushed the pile of sand into it. Once it was full, I sat right on top of it and fell back to look up into the sky. Sandpipers were darting back and forth above me; the occasional one swooped into the waves, trying to catch small fish that washed up on shore.

I reached into my back pocket when my cell phone vibrated. After brushing some sand off of it, I read what was on the screen. I rolled my eyes and scoffed in disgust after reading the text message. "Nosey ass," I mumbled. It was from Jordan; he wanted to know where I was and when I'd bring his lunch. I texted back, "Nowhere special" and "Soon" and then shoved the phone back into my pocket as I sat up. No one, except Alexia and Julian, knew I went to the beach a few days a week. They had promised to keep it a secret. They didn't laugh or judge me when I told them about what I was doing there, so it was nice to know that I was able to confide in them.

I fished my phone out of my pocket again when it vibrated a second time. This time, Jordan asked what time "soon" would be. I stared at the screen blankly. I wanted to send him something that I knew would piss him off but changed my mind. Running errands and doing favors for him so I didn't have to hear how neglectful I was being toward him since Alexia's accident was starting to get old. When he first made that accusation, I almost laughed in his face; but I had controlled the urge. Lately, he had been working on my last nerve. I wasn't sure how much longer I was going to be able to take it.

2

As I wiggled my toes in the sand, I looked out into the ocean. The emerald-blue color of it always put me into a trance and at ease whenever I saw it. I didn't want to leave, but duty called. After grabbing my flip-flops, notebook, and pen, I rose to my feet and made my way back to the parking lot. I looked back to the ocean when I got to the top of a small sand dune, remembering that I'd be back later that week, if not the next day.

I tossed the notebook and pen into the passenger seat of my car on top of my purse and got settled in the driver's seat. I took note of the time when the radio on the dashboard lights came on. I hadn't realized that it was so late in the afternoon, which made my heart sink. "Great . . . he'll be angry with me, I'm sure." I threw the car in reverse to make my way to the nearest store to grab a premade sub, soda, and dessert.

After grabbing Jordan's lunch, which included some extra cookies in hopes that they would help me avoid an argument with him, I sped to his place of employment. He worked at a family-owned auto parts store as the manager. From what I gathered, he enjoyed his job very much, most likely because he was paid handsomely to boss people around. His family had opened the store a few years back when they came into some money. Ever since then, Jordan had had this sense of entitlement that he flaunted without hesitation. He claimed that being in charge of others was what he did best.

I parked next to Jordan's truck around the side of the store and quickly jumped out. I checked my phone for the time and silently hoped he was too busy to notice that I was late by half an hour. Without warning, the sub fell out of the bag and onto the ground as soon as I started a brisk walk to the front of the building. "*Seriously?*" I moaned and closed my eyes as I dropped my head back so I was looking up at the sky. After a moment or two of staring at a few birds coast by, I stooped over and scooped up the sub. Part of me was relieved that it had been wrapped in paper after the deli employee had made it, but the other part of me wouldn't have cared if it hadn't been. I would have given it to him anyway, dirt and all.

I brushed it off quickly and shoved it back into the small plastic bag. "I don't even know why I still bother trying to do something nice for someone so ungrateful." I started walking again as I fought to tie a knot in the handles of the plastic bag so the sub wouldn't fall out again. I was so busy paying attention to what I was doing that I bumped into someone before I could look up.

"Who's ungrateful?"

I took a step back and found Jordan standing in front of me. He crossed his arms over his crisp dress shirt as he waited for an answer. I exhaled deeply from my nose and was ready to scream at the top of my lungs, but I decided not to waste my time, or my breath. "No one in particular," I responded curtly.

"Where were you this whole time? You're late with my lunch; I was beginning to worry." He took the bag out of my hand, untied the poorly done knot, and fished the bottle of soda out of it. He twisted the top off and took a drink.

"You were beginning to worry about *me*?"

"No; I was worried I may not have anything for lunch," Jordan snickered.

"Figures." I rolled my eyes and crossed my arms.

"Where were you?" he questioned again.

"Nowhere special," I answered for what felt like the millionth time that day.

"That's not a good enough answer." Jordan twisted the top back onto the soda and looked at me as if I were covering something up.

"Well, that answer will have to do. I said 'nowhere special' and I meant just that. What more do you want?" I could feel myself growing agitated.

"What I want is for you to be on time with my lunch." He leaned in close to my face and tapped the face of his watch.

"But I'm on time every *other* day to bring your stupid lunch, except today," I pointed out. "Don't *those* days count for anything?" I peered around him when I noticed one of his employees coming around the corner from the front of the store.

"Excuse me, Jordan?" the employee waited for Jordan to acknowledge him.

Jordan turned away from me and smiled at him. "Yes?"

"Your dad called; I've placed him on hold. He's ready when you are," he informed him. He peeked around Jordan and gave a nervous wave. "Afternoon, Alora," he said with an anxious smile.

I smiled as well and waved in return as he turned away from us to make his way back inside. Jordan turned back to me as he began digging in his pants pocket. "Here, buy yourself something to eat, and grab a movie or two so you have something to keep you occupied when you get home. It's my treat. I'll come by after work, so pick up something good." He pulled out a hundred dollar bill and handed it to me. I took it with a sigh and shoved it in my front pocket. "Hey, I said I'd be over later," he reiterated. "Now, like I said, on your way home, grab something to eat and get a few movies." Jordan spun me around, gave me a gentle push toward my car, and made his way inside so he could take the important call that was waiting for him.

"You're welcome for the lunch," I mumbled. Shaking my head as I got back into my car, I pulled the money he had given me out of my pocket. "A hundred dollars—who cares?" I reached under my seat and pulled out a small, wooden keepsake box with my initials, "AP," engraved in the lid. It was a gift that Jordan had given to me when we first started dating during our junior year in high school. I opened the box and dropped the crisp bill inside along with the rest of the money he had given me over the past three months. What I'd do with it, I wasn't sure; there had to be well over fifteen hundred dollars in there. I shut the lid, shoved it back under the seat, and headed home. I didn't think twice about him coming by when he got off of work for the day. Every time he said he would, he was late or didn't stay long. I hated his lack of punctuality *so much. There's no way I can continue going through this with him,* I thought. *At some point, I've got to put my foot down before this gets more out of hand than it already has.*

—Chapter 2—

Unexpected traffic made it feel like it took forever to get from Jordan's job to my apartment. By the time I got home, I was tired and more frustrated than I had originally been. After making sure the money I was stashing in the car was secure under the driver's seat, I made my way up two flights of stairs to my place. Once inside, I shut the door quietly behind me and tossed my keys into a small bowl that sat on a nearby table. As I walked to my bedroom, I pulled out my cell phone to check and see if I had received any texts or calls while I was driving. It didn't surprise me that I hadn't. I slipped out of my flip-flops as I swapped my phone for the TV remote. I cut on the television and tried to relax after flopping onto my bed. Minutes after an unsuccessful search for a show to watch, I popped a DVD into the player beside the TV. Before I knew it, my eyelids were growing heavy, and minutes into the movie, I fell asleep.

My eyes shot open when I heard shuffling coming from the hallway outside of my bedroom. It was dark, and the TV was off. I sat up and eyed the empty doorway silently as I waited to see if I'd hear the shuffling a second time. Once my eyes adjusted after staring out into the dark hallway for a minute, I noticed that something small was sitting in the doorway. It shook violently and rose to its feet. I smiled as I swung my legs over the side of the bed. "Come here, Raven." I patted my knee for my small, jet-black Labrador puppy to hear. She scampered to me quickly and put her front paws on my knees. "How's my girl?"

I scooped her up and cradled her in my arms as I stood, grabbed my phone, and carried her out of the room with me. I had adopted her from a local shelter as a gift to myself. I needed company in some way, shape, or form, so I figured adopting a puppy was the answer. Since she hadn't greeted me at the door when I got home like she usually did, I knew she was asleep somewhere in the apartment and didn't disturb her. I knew she'd come looking for me when she woke up.

I took her into the kitchen and sat her on the floor closest to the sink after I cut on the overhead light. "It's dinner time, Raven," I chirped happily. I went into the cabinet under the sink, opened the bag of puppy food, and scooped some into her small food bowl. I noticed I had two missed calls as I sat it on the floor in front of her. I called my voice mail box and let the messages play as I watched her eat. The first message was from Jordan; he was letting me know that he wouldn't be coming by. "Well, that doesn't surprise me in the slightest." I snickered as I rolled my eyes. The second message was from Alexia. She wanted me to join her and Julian for lunch the next day. I picked up the food bowl when Raven was finished, rinsed it out in the sink, and then gave the bowl back to her with water in it. She drank it happily.

When Raven finished the water, I took the bowl and placed it back under the sink. She barked playfully as she vaulted into the front room to grab her large stuffed toy. She was swinging it wildly and banging it against the couch. I yawned loudly as I deleted the voice mails from my phone and made my way back to my room. Once there, I fell back into the softness of my bed. I crawled under the blankets—still fully dressed—and drifted back to sleep. I had had a long, frustrating day, which was just like any other day since I had started dating Jordan. At the *end* of the day, though, there was nothing like a good night's sleep to be reenergized for a brand new one.

My eyes shot open a second time to the sound of the doorbell ringing; only this time, the sun was pouring into the bedroom through the blinds. Raven was sound asleep at the end of the bed. I slowly slipped out of the bed so I wouldn't wake her and made my way to the front door. I moaned as I rubbed my right eye, brushed my hair back from my face, and then wiped my right cheek. The doorbell rang again just as I looked through the peephole. The visitor's back was to the door, but I knew who it was. I unlocked the door and opened it slowly. She turned around quickly to face me.

"Afternoon, sleepyhead." It was Alexia, chipper and ready to go as usual. "Did you get my message last night?" She reached out and removed a small downy feather that had come from my pillow and stuck to my eyelash.

I yawned and stretched as I leaned lazily against the door frame. "Yes, Alex," I mumbled drowsily. "Lunch with you and Jules today. I got it." I rolled off of the door frame back into the apartment and motioned for her come inside. "Where is he, anyway? You two are usually attached at the hip," I joked.

She shut the door behind herself and followed me to my room. "He said he'd meet us there. He's going to secure a booth for us. Where's Raven?" She glanced around the front room and into the kitchen.

"Sleeping." I pointed her out once we got into my room and slowly began to leaf through my closet in an effort to find something to wear. "You didn't have any trouble getting up the stairs, did you?" I asked. Alex was still going through physical therapy because of her leg injury from the car accident she had been in during our freshman year. A pipe had gone through her left thigh, and she had a hairline fracture in the same leg. But because she was going to therapy regularly, and had Jules's help, she was healing quickly and was back on her feet in no time.

Alex slowly sat on the bed so she wouldn't wake Raven and looked on. "Not really. I mean, stairs have gotten much easier to take, but it was still a bit of a struggle. I should be 100 percent by the time we start school again. At least that's what the therapist told me."

"That's good to hear."

I thought that it'd take at *least* four summer sessions for Alex to catch up because she was out for the entire spring semester following the accident. How she was able to catch up in just two summer sessions was beyond me. But by the end of the fall semester of our sophomore year, she was caught up. I was happy that she wouldn't need to take classes this summer so she could relax and enjoy the break before our junior year began.

I grabbed a sundress and a pair of matching sandals to wear with it and then closed the closet door after I gently laid the clothes on the bed. "Hey, while I'm getting ready, could you be *super* awesome and feed Raven a cup of puppy food from under the sink and then take her out? That way we can leave as soon as I'm done getting dressed. If taking her for a walk will be too much for you, I understand."

"She's not a puller, is she? I should be fine if she isn't."

"She's pretty well behaved when she goes for walks. If she's not, just shout at her and she'll settle down. I don't think you'll have any problems, though."

"Sure, I can do that. Where's her leash?"

"It's in the bowl by the front door with my car keys." I watched as Alex slowly got to her feet. She winced as she put her weight on her left leg. "Alex, if your leg is bothering you—"

"Alora, I said I'd do it. *Please* don't baby me; I get enough of that from Jules and my parents."

"Okay, sorry. I'll be ready in a few minutes."

"Take your time."

She gave me a stern but thoughtful look, and then made her way out to the kitchen. I listened as she rummaged under the sink, grabbed the aluminum dog food bowl, and scooped food into it as I started the shower. The moment the food hit the bowl, Raven shot up from her sleep and sped out to the kitchen to eat. I heard Alex giggle as I shut the bedroom door so I could get ready to head out for the day.

After freshening up, fixing my hair, and getting dressed, I exited the bathroom with the towel I used in hand. Alex was playing with Raven in the middle of the bed. They both seemed to be enjoying themselves. I smirked as I folded the towel and draped it over the footboard. "Okay, you two, I have to make the bed."

They both stopped and looked at me. Alex got up slowly; Raven jumped to the floor and ran out to the front room. "You were right; she's well behaved when she's taken for her walk. I didn't have any issues with her. You're training her pretty well."

"Good. That means I'm doing *something* right around here." I tossed the large blue blanket in the air and let it land over the mattress lightly.

"What's that supposed to mean?"

I thought about what had happened the day before with Jordan at his job and quickly dismissed it. "Nothing. I'll be ready to go after I do this." I smoothed the blanket out with both hands and sat my pillows on top. After making the bed, I closed the blinds slightly, made sure the light was off in the bathroom, and checked to make sure the bathroom door was closed all the way so Raven couldn't get in. Alex followed me as I walked around the apartment to make sure everything else was in order before walking out the door. I checked the kitchen last to make sure the cabinet where the puppy food was kept was closed tightly and then cracked the blinds that looked out to the front of the apartment complex. I turned the TV on and changed the channel to Animal Planet. "Raven, baby," I called. She ran toward me from under a chair that was on the other side of the room with her stuffed toy in her mouth. "Look here, sweetie." I pointed to the TV as a dog show came back on from commercial break. She dropped the stuffed toy and sat down, watching it excitedly.

"Did you train her to do that too?" Alex asked while opening the front door.

"No, she likes watching other dogs on TV. Crazy, right?" I bent over and scratched Raven between the ears. "Be good." She kept watching TV as I grabbed my purse, and followed Alex outside. I locked the door behind me and gave it a gentle push to make sure it was secure. "Who's driving?"

"I'll drive; I don't mind." She walked by me and made her way to the stairwell to head down to the parking lot.

"Do you want me to—"

"I've taken these stairs three times today. I'll be okay walking down first."

Although she said she'd be okay, I followed close behind her as we made our descent. She gripped the railing as she pushed herself to walk at normal speed. Surprisingly, she didn't stumble or complain about any pain she may have been having. I expected her to at least curse under her breath, but she was too busy talking about the classes she planned on enrolling in for the fall. "Have you decided on any of *your* classes yet?" Alex asked as she fumbled through her purse to find her keys. She slowly made her way around the bend in the stairwell to go down the last set of stairs.

"Ugh . . . do we *have* to talk about this right now?"

"I'm going with Jules to the campus to enroll tomorrow," she replied. "You were supposed to have at least four classes chosen so you could come with us and get it out of the way. You know they fill up pretty fast. You don't want to end up in crap classes, do you?" she said coolly, looking back to me as she stepped onto the sidewalk with a smirk.

"If by crap classes you mean *not* taking elementary Spanish with you, no, I don't," I sighed.

"Then if I were you, I'd sit down tonight, go through the course catalog, and figure out what you want to enroll in besides that one. We're going first thing in the morning."

She unlocked her car as we approached it. It was a newer model of the one she had gotten into the accident with. She refused to get a car that was bigger or smaller than the old one; she loved *that* particular model that much. If she could have, she would have had someone fix the old one so she'd still have it. The license plate frame with her family nickname, *Marbles,* and colorful cat's-eye marbles surrounding the name shone brightly in the sun. Jules managed to get a replacement one for her while she was in the hospital.

We got inside and buckled our seat belts. "Jules noticed that you've been down in the dumps lately, so we figured we'd take you somewhere special—our treat." Alex checked behind her multiple times before backing out of the parking space. Since the accident, she was more alert when she drove. We never told her she was being overly cautious; if anything, we were just as cautious when we were with her.

"I *have* been a little stressed," I said as I looked out my window behind us as well to give her the extra okay she needed to know that it was safe to back out. When I looked back to her, she was staring at me with a goofy look on her face. I burst out laughing. She always found the craziest ways to make me smile.

"I knew I still had it." She put the car in reverse and backed out slowly. "Come on. Whatever's bothering you can't be *that* bad." She elbowed me in my arm as she began to drive us to our destination. "It could be worse, you know?"

"Yeah, you're right," I agreed.

—Chapter 3—

We pulled into the parking lot of a seafood restaurant that many of the college students frequented. It had taken everything in me to not let a past incident that the four of us had gotten into almost two years ago taint my love for the place. I had never gotten to apologize to Jules for Jordan's behavior. As Jordan and I were leaving on the night of said incident, we passed by Alex and Jules; they were waiting for a table to be free so they could be seated. Jordan decided to exchange a few words with Jules, which almost ended in a huge physical altercation. Jordan swore he was in the right, but I knew he wasn't. I was glad the owner of the place noticed what was happening and stepped in to stop it.

Once Alex parked next to Jules's car, we headed inside. "Surprised?" she inquired as we walked side by side.

"I'm more pleased than anything. You know, I never apologized to Jules for what had happened that one night awhile back."

"It's water under the bridge. Besides, you can't apologize for Jordan's behavior. I've told you that before. He's got a mind of his own, just like you. Jules isn't thinking about it anymore anyway. In fact, after you two left that night, we didn't speak of it again. He's pretty good at letting things go."

"If a fight *did* break out, though, who do you think would have won?" I whispered as we walked past a small group of people that was leaving the restaurant.

"Jordan has Jules in size—there's no doubt about that. But I'd put my money on Jules," she said with a smile. "I'm not saying that because I know him. I'm saying that because deep down in my heart of hearts, I think he could take Jordan if he had to. You know what they say about the quiet ones."

I remembered how Jordan had called Jules by the wrong name multiple times that night; Jules calmly corrected him each time. And when he actually insulted Jordan, he did it seamlessly while showing no emotion. He didn't even flinch when Jordan advanced toward him. The only person who had moved when Jordan advanced was Alex, and that was to get in between them. I doubted that she would have been able to stop either of them if a fight had actually ensued, but I admired her for stepping up that night.

We walked up a small set of steps and entered through the double doors up to the seating podium. The host nodded to us kindly and led us to a booth located by a window that looked out to the inlet. While following him, I looked around and noticed how many of the patrons were couples sitting at tables for two or large groups of couples sitting at oversized tables. My stomach churned at the very sight of it. It also made me despise Jordan even more. I looked ahead to watch where I was going and acted like I didn't see anyone else around me.

The host placed three menus on the table and then walked away as Jules slid out of the booth to greet us. He gave me a hug and then hugged Alex. She slid into the booth when he stepped to the side. He then slid in next to her as I took a seat across from them. I didn't bother to open a menu like they did because I already knew what I wanted to order. They quickly made their selections and placed their menus back on the table.

"What're you two getting?" I asked.

Alex pushed their menus to the middle of the table. "I'm getting the usual."

"Raw clams?" I guessed, placing my menu on top of hers.

"Of course."

"What about you, Jules?"

"Fried eel," he smirked.

"Ewlk."

"You know, Alex said the same thing the first time we ate here together. I still can't get her to try it."

"And you never will," she laughed.

I looked out of the window at the choppy water and watched as a small boat tugged by. It was beautiful out; I was glad they had gotten me out my apartment for the day.

"So how's the job hunt going?" Jules asked me.

I snapped out of my trance and sighed as I slouched in the booth. "I haven't had much luck finding anything." I started to poke at my silverware wrapped in a crisp red napkin.

"I keep telling you, you should work with me at the diner," Alex suggested. "I saw how you balanced all those items without strain at the hospital that one day. I'm still trying to control not dropping empty carrying trays."

"Or I could talk to the owner here and see if there are any openings," Jules chimed in.

"Thanks, but with Jordan paying for just about everything, I really don't *need* a job. I'm just trying to find one so I have something to do," I said with a scowl. I was grateful for Jordan's financial help but not at what it was costing me emotionally.

"Right," Jules said quietly. "How's Raven?"

"She's good. You'd think I paid for her to go to obedience school; she's *that* well behaved," I answered.

"Yeah, she's a real sweetheart," Alex added.

"Well, that's good. At least she keeps you company—not like Jordan." Jules sneered when he said his name. Alex elbowed him, and he looked at her in confusion. "What? It's true," he protested. "Don't act like I'm not stating facts."

"He's right, Alex," I said in his defense.

"I know that." She pinched Jules's arm lightly, causing him to jump. "That doesn't mean we need to discuss it. It may summon him; we don't want that," she whispered with a light laugh.

Jules stuck his tongue out at Alex and smiled. As much as I loathed seeing happy couples, I couldn't when it came to them—*if* they were a couple. I just safely assumed that they were an item since one was rarely seen without the other—that and he bought necklaces and charms for the two of them while she was in the hospital. The charms were uppercase letters that were the same style and cut. The only difference was that hers was a gold letter *A* and his was a silver letter *J*. That seemed like more than a friendly gesture to me. But, regardless of what they were to each other, they were lucky to *have* each other, even if they were just very close friends.

I dug into my purse when my phone began to ring. I knew it was Jordan because of the ringtone that was playing for the call. I answered it while Alex and Jules talked quietly amongst themselves. "Hello?"

"Where are you?" Jordan asked.

"I'm out with Alex and Jules."

"Doing what?"

"Waiting to place my order. They're treating me to lunch."

He fell silent. All I could hear was the telephone ringing in the background of his small office. I waited a few more seconds and was about to say something, but he beat me to the punch. "We need to talk."

"Can't it wait until after I eat?"

"No, it can't. We need to talk *now*."

"If this is about what you want for lunch later—"

"I don't think we should see each other anymore."

My breath caught in my throat when I heard those words. Any other person who was as annoyed as I was with the relationship would have been thrilled. But I only felt anger and confusion. "I don't understand. When did you decide this?" I was ready to start shouting at the top of my lungs.

"Does it really matter?"

He was notorious for answering my questions with a question. He knew it irked me, but he did it anyway. "Of course it matters," I said as calmly as I could.

"Listen, don't act like any of this is coming as a surprise to you. You should have known it'd happen eventually."

"You were getting practically everything you could possibly want from me," I responded. "How was I supposed to know I'd get blindsided like this?"

"With the way you've been acting ever since Alexia was in that accident, anyone could see it was coming.

25

It became painfully obvious where your loyalties lie the minute you chose to spend a good portion of your time at that hospital. Then there's your poor choice of company once she was released—"

"My friends are *not* a poor choice in company. If anything, staying with *you* for as long as I did was a poor choice," I said through clenched teeth as I continued to try and stay calm.

"Whose fault is that, then? Not mine. It was *your* choice to hang around and mooch off of *me*."

How could he say something like that to me? I thought. *After everything I did for him, after everything he put me through.* I looked across the table and noticed that Alex had been staring at me the entire time I was on the phone. I gently pushed a button on the side of it to lower the volume in case what Jordan was saying could be heard. Jules was still talking to her as he flipped through the menu again, but she continued eyeing me as if he wasn't there with us. It was almost as though she was trying to read me. Her face looked the same way I felt—sick and angry. Jules stopped talking when he realized she wasn't responding to him and looked at me as well. A look of confusion formed on his face as I began to wrap up the call.

"I started dating you *before* your parents came into that money and opened that store of theirs. You *know*

that. But, hey, if this is what you think needs to be done."
I tried to sound indifferent.

"So you're okay with this then?" he inquired.

"Sure. I mean, you *only* called and did this over
the phone, in the middle of me spending time with my
friends," I said sarcastically. "How am I supposed to be
okay with *any* of this?"

"Alora," Jordan sighed in exasperation, "you seem to
be confused as to how a breakup is supposed to work.
I ended our relationship, right? So, you're supposed to
accept it, say something mean, maybe cry a little, and
then hang up on me. But if you still aren't getting this,
I can explain it to you again; only this time, I'll speak
slower so you'll understand."

My blood pressure rose with every insult he was
throwing at me. It wasn't right out there in the open, but
he had a way of making me feel inferior without coming
right out and saying the harsh words that would shut any
conversation down. "You're so full of yourself, you know
that?" I grumbled into the phone. "You said it's over, so
that's it. It's over."

"*Finally,*" he said curtly. "Have fun with your misfit
friends."

"Whatever."

I took the phone away from my ear and hung up. My hand was shaking from being upset, so I placed the phone on the table instead of back in my purse. I really wanted to chuck it through the window into the inlet, but then I would have had to buy another phone—and pay for the damaged window. I wiped my eyes to try and stop the developing tears from rolling down my face and sat up straight. "The waiter sure is taking a long time to come back to take our orders," I said as I fought to keep my voice from cracking.

"Alora, who was that?" Alex asked.

I waved my hand to flag down a waiter and one came toward us. He stood patiently at the end of the table and waited for us to order. Alex continued to stare at me the same way she had been when I was on the phone, which was starting to weird me out. I grabbed all three menus off of the table and shoved them at the waiter. "I'll take a root beer and two dozen raw clams on the half shell. If you could bring an extra bowl of sliced lemons to dress them with, that'd be great. Alex plans on ordering the same, so we'll need the extra slices."

The waiter quickly jotted down my order after taking the menus out of my hand. I slipped away from the table to go to the restroom when Jules began to place his order. After walking quickly through the sea of waiters and waitresses, I pushed through the bathroom door. It closed quietly behind me as I covered my mouth to hold in the loud sob that wanted to emit from it. I didn't know if I was alone in the bathroom, so I didn't want to embarrass myself. I walked into the handicap stall, gripped the sink, and squeezed my eyes closed as tightly as I possibly could. After taking a moment, I exhaled loudly and opened my eyes. "I can't believe it's over because *he* made the decision. It was supposed to be *mine!*"

—Chapter 4—

The harder I tried to keep myself from crying, the more I felt ready to explode. I could feel my nose burning from trying to hold the tears back for so long. I sighed and shut my eyes again. "I *knew* I shouldn't have hesitated to do something about this," I whispered. Tears finally began to slowly stream down my face. They landed on the porcelain sink; the quiet pitter-patter echoed quietly in the stall. My eyes flew open when I heard someone walk into the bathroom. I quickly turned on the faucet, and splashed my face with cold water to hide that I was crying. When I felt a hand on my shoulder, I looked behind me and found Alex standing there. I turned back to the sink and sniffled as I snatched a paper towel from the dispenser and blotted my face dry.

"Alora, who called you?" She looked at my reflection in the mirror and waited for an answer.

I looked at her reflection in the mirror as well and just stared.

"Who was it?" she asked again.

I looked away as I shook my head.

"Was it Jordan?"

"Yup."

"What did he say?" She closed the stall door and then stood next to me at the sink.

I shook my head again and continued to wipe my face.

"Alora, *talk* to me."

I turned to face her after shutting the water off as I took a deep breath and tried to keep myself from crying again. "He called to tell me that he didn't think we should be seeing each other anymore."

"Oh . . . well, not to sound unsympathetic or anything, but I'd think that's something you'd be happy about. You've been trying to figure out how to get out of that relationship for a while now." She pulled her phone out of her pocket and unlocked it. Her fingers moved quickly across the screen as she composed what I assumed was a text message.

"Right. *I* was trying to find a way out of it. He had no reason to make the first move seeing as how I didn't do anything wrong. *He* was the issue, not me."

"Soooo . . . are you more upset that he beat you to the punch or that you got dumped?"

"It's hard to say. I want to say the former and not the latter. It's not like I knew when I was going to make the move myself anyway. Who're you texting?"

"No one. I'm sorry." Alex tried to hide what seemed to be a hint of excitement as she looked up from her phone. She hit the lock button at the top of it and shoved it back into her pocket.

I turned on the water again and splashed some on my face one last time, and then I grabbed a new paper towel to dry off. When I was finished, I balled it up, tossed it into the trash can, and then cut the water off. "You're right. I should be happy regardless of who did the actual dumping. I just hate thinking I'll look like the one that deserved it when other people find out."

"Trust me—the entire campus saw the way he conducted himself when he was with you. If they even care that this happened, they know it wasn't because of something *you* did. They'd have to be blind, deaf, and stupid to assume otherwise." She pulled me in so she could give me a hug. I hugged her back until she took a step away from me.

"At least I still have Raven," I tried to convince myself.

"And me, Jules, Matt, and Samantha," Alex pointed out.

"Right."

"Besides, you don't need Jordan. You never did. Trust me, someone will come along soon enough, and you'll be saying 'Jordan who?' Until then, though, you know we don't mind you tagging along with us if you ever want some company. Or, I can break away from Jules and we can have one-on-one time like the good old days. You know he won't mind."

"I couldn't do that," I said as she led us out of the bathroom stall.

"You can, and will, if you need to." Alex continued to lead the way back to the table after she opened the bathroom door and held it for me. From a distance, I could see Jules talking to one of the waiters. Alex must have seen that too because she slowed her pace and fell back so we were walking next to each other. "Want to get some air real quick?"

"Yeah, sure."

We stepped outside and stood to the side of the double doors. The summer heat felt good on my face after splashing all of that cold water on it. The smell of freshly cut grass filled my nose as I inhaled deeply. We cracked a couple of jokes for a few minutes as people passed by to go inside. Once I was feeling better, we went back in to sit down. As we approached the table, we noticed that our food still hadn't arrived.

"Everything okay?" Jules asked Alex as she slid back into the booth next to him.

"It is now," she answered.

"I wonder what's taking our food so long to get here." I slid into the seat across from them and took a sip of what had become warm root beer. I made a face and pushed it away.

"The waiter brought it out while you two were in the restroom, so I had him take it back and hold it so it wouldn't get cold—warm in your and Alex's case," he chuckled.

Minutes after we sat back down, the waiter brought our food out to us. We took our time to eat and chatted for a good portion of the afternoon. It felt good to sit and listen to the both of them tell stories and joke around with each other.

"Tell Alora about where Benny just recently went." Jules grabbed his soda and finished the last of it.

"Iceland. He said he wanted to get an amazing tan while he was there." Alex took my plate and placed it on top of hers in the middle of the table, and then she placed them both on top of Jules's empty plate.

"Why does Benny go to the most ridiculous places to do the most inaccurate things?" I laughed.

"Listen, you're asking the wrong person," Alex shrugged. "I'll be sure to let him know you're wondering about his travels when he comes back to visit."

After holding small talk and listening to more of Alex's ridiculous stories for a few more hours, Jules walked us to her car after paying for our food. "Did you want to come by and watch a couple of movies with us?" he offered. "I picked up a pretty good DVD selection from the flea market last weekend on the way home from work."

"Nah, I should really get home to Raven and make sure she's okay. I don't like leaving her alone for too long. Plus, I have some things to figure out in regard to my living arrangement, and I have to pick my classes so I can register for them tomorrow morning with you guys."

"Well, just give Alex a call and let her know you're heading over if you change your mind." He leaned in and gave me a hug. "I'll see *you* in a bit." He pointed to Alex and winked as he walked away and got into his car. We watched as he pulled out of the parking lot and headed to his apartment.

Alex took her time driving back to my place. When we got there, we sat in the parking lot for a bit and went over a few of the issues I'd have to figure out before things started to crumble from beneath me. Jordan had been paying my rent and supplying me with food for myself and Raven. It was safe to assume that since we were no longer together, I'd have to scramble to find a job so I could support myself. It wasn't that I didn't want to work; it was just difficult to find anything that paid enough to stay afloat.

"Your rent is due in a few weeks; will you be able to pay it?" Alex unbuckled her seat belt so she could get more comfortable.

"I should be covered until I can find a job."

"What about having food to eat?"

"I should be covered until I can find a job," I repeated.

"And Raven?"

"She's taken care of for a while too," I sighed. "Jordan used to give me 'just because' money. I never used it. I always stashed it for emergency purposes. I'm sure I have well over fifteen hundred dollars."

"Smart thinking," Alex praised.

"I guess I should take it out of my car and count it tonight or something."

"Seriously, Alora?" She pushed me on my shoulder. "It's not safe to keep it in your car. You need to take that cash into your apartment."

"I know, I know. I've been meaning to. It just always slips my mind." I dug into my purse and pulled out my keys.

"Well, you know that I'll help you find a job if you're still having problems finding one on your own. Jules is more than willing to help, too. If worse comes to worse, you can always go back to your parents until you find something, right?"

"No. Not because they won't take me back in, because they will. I just refuse to start from square one. I'll figure something out; I always do."

I glanced at the radio as Alex turned the car on and noticed that it was still pretty early in the evening. A part of me wanted to change my mind and ride with her to Jules's place to watch movies like he had originally offered. But after giving it some careful thought, I knew I had to stick with my original plan and figure out my current situation first. I slid out of the passenger seat and closed the door as she rolled down the window.

"Remember, if you change your mind about coming over, just give me a call. You know you're more than welcome to join us," she reminded me.

"I will. I promise."

I watched as she slowly backed out of the parking spot after putting on her seat belt and making absolutely sure no one was coming. She waved to me as she pulled away, and I waved to her until she was no longer in sight. I made my way over to my car to get the cash from under the seat before heading up to check on Raven. As I got closer, I noticed that something was off about it. The driver's side door looked as though it wasn't closed all the way, and the interior lights were on. My stomach sank when I looked through the window and saw the spare key to my apartment and car on the front seat. *Jordan must have stopped by on his break to return them and didn't realize he didn't close the door all the way,* I thought. *Please let the money still be under the seat . . .*

I unlocked the car, shoved the spare keys into my purse, and frantically felt under the car seat. For a brief moment, I didn't feel my keepsake box. I was overwhelmed with relief when my fingers finally touched the cool engraved lid. Happy that nothing had happened to it, I pulled it from under the seat and hugged it against my chest as I got to my feet. Then, I made sure the car would start since I didn't know how long the interior lights had been on because the door was cracked. After it started successfully on the first try, I locked it and headed up to my apartment.

Raven greeted me happily when I entered by jumping all over me as I worked to get my feet out of my sandals. I dropped my keys into the bowl by the front door and sat my purse on the kitchen counter. After I put the keepsake box on the dining room table, I stooped down and scratched Raven behind her ears. She fell over and lay on the carpet as she yelped and whined excitedly. "Someone is happy I'm home," I laughed. I took her for a quick walk after slipping into a pair of flip-flops and then fed her before sitting down to count the money in the box to see how soon I'd have to secure a job. After checking my phone for messages, I sat it down as I took a seat at the dining room table. I pulled the box closer to me and opened it, only to freeze and stare blankly inside of it. I pulled out a small, folded piece of paper as I tried to control my hands from shaking and read the contents of the handwritten note:

You can keep the box, but you can't keep the cash.
—Jordan

I stared at the note a second longer, and then I slowly folded it back up and dropped it back inside. After gently closing the lid, I picked up the box and chucked it across the room as hard as I could while screaming at the top of my lungs. It hit the wall, which caused the lid to separate from the base. Both pieces flew in separate directions and left a dent in the wall. Raven walked up to me slowly and nudged my leg with her cold, wet nose.

"Not now, Raven," I growled.

She nudged me again and whimpered.

"Not now, Raven!"

She yelped and ran away from me to hide beneath the armchair in the front room. Once there, she didn't make another sound.

After spacing out for an hour and allowing myself to calm down, I went and found both pieces of the box. The base of it was okay, but the lid was slightly cracked from the impact. I sat both pieces on the coffee table and then went to apologize to Raven. It wasn't her fault that the money I needed for the both of us was gone. She could sense that I was upset and had just wanted to try and make things better. I felt bad that I had yelled at her the way I had. I got on my hands and knees and looked under the armchair where she was hiding. She was as far to the back as she could possibly get so she couldn't be reached. She looked at me sadly as I lay on my stomach and reached for her.

"I'm sorry, Raven. I didn't mean to yell at you. Want to come out now? We can go to the beach for a while and play," I offered.

Still not moving an inch, she looked at me and sniffed the air.

"I'll get you a cookie," I bribed.

When she heard the word *cookie*, her ears perked up.

"You know you want a tasty treat. How about *two* cookies? I'll give you one for behaving while I was out and one because I wrongfully yelled at you. That sounds nice, right?"

I got to my feet and made my way to the kitchen. I listened as she slowly shuffled her way out from under the chair while I dug into the dog treat bag. By the time I grabbed the two I had promised her and turned around, she was sitting at my feet, wagging her tail intensely. I picked her up, carried her over to the couch, and fed them to her one by one after I sat down. She ate them quickly and then curled up in my lap. She was either very good at forgiving people, or she had a very short-term memory when treats were involved.

"Well, Raven, we're in a bit of a pickle," I sighed. "I thought I'd be able to take care of us for at *least* two months, but that plan backfired. I shouldn't have left that money in the car. That wasn't smart of me at all." Raven nipped at my fingers as I talked to her. I had offered to take her to the beach, so I decided that maybe getting some fresh air and playing fetch with her would clear my head. I placed her on the floor, led her to the front door, clipped the leash onto her collar, and grabbed my car keys along with my purse. After slipping my sandals back on, I walked out, locked the door behind me, and then led her down to the car. She jumped into the passenger seat and stuck her head out of the window after I got in and rolled it down for her.

"Don't worry. This is only a minor setback," I told her. I sent a quick text to Alex telling her what had happened and where I was going, and then I dropped the phone into the cup holder in the center console. "I'll figure out how to make things right." I pulled out of the parking spot and headed to the beach, trying everything in my power to hash out a solution in my mind on the way.

—Chapter 5—

"Don't be that way, James." Jules sat across from me on the arm of one of my loveseats. "I'll stop by later and tell you how she's doing. You know that."

"I don't know how much longer I'll be able to sit around here and do nothing. I can't help but feel as though I got the short end of the stick when I agreed to do this nearly two years ago," I said grudgingly.

I was on the verge of causing Alora and Jordan to break up if one of them didn't do it themselves. It felt as though ages had passed since I was put on project Get Alora to Leave Jordan. That's what I called it at least.

There wasn't much else I *could* call it; the name fit the description to a T.

I was in the middle of reading one of my favorite pieces that Alora had written and buried at the beach when Jules stopped by. She had written a poem the same day that Alex regained consciousness in the hospital. When Jules learned that she was going to the beach that night when visiting hours were over, he told me. So I patiently waited in my car among other parked cars that were there before going to the hospital to visit Alex myself. I watched from a distance as Alora walked onto the beach. After she was out of sight, I walked onto the beach as well and sat with a group that was gathered around a bonfire so I could continue to watch her. I remember thinking that she may have caught me when she paused from reading out loud what she had written to look around briefly. I was relieved when she went back to what she was doing. When she was finished, she buried the poem and then headed home soon after. I didn't have to wait for a colorful seashell to wash up on shore and rest on top of the burial spot to know where it was.

When Jules came in and seated himself, I put the poem back into the small wooden box where I kept all of her writings that I collected from the beach. I asked if he wanted to do anything that day, and he informed me that he already had plans with Alex to treat Alora to lunch since she seemed a little down in the dumps. He was just stopping by until it was time to head to the restaurant.

"I'm tired of waiting around idly while you guys report what's going on with her *for* me. Whenever the three of you hang out, it's breaking news with Alexia Waters and Julian Reed. It was easier to bear when it was just *you* telling me what was going on with Alora."

Jules gave me a stern look.

"That came out wrong. I'm sorry. I'm just getting restless. You two keep telling me that she's tired of Jordan, but she's *still* letting him hang around. What's the holdup?"

"You can't rush this sort of thing." Jules pulled his phone out of his back pocket and checked it. "Alex said she'd do anything to help you, and that's exactly what she's doing. She knows you don't like not being able to take action, and *maybe* she can get Alora's situation to change sooner than expected. Don't you have some designs to sketch for work? I'm almost positive I gave you a bunch of orders from the jobs website last weekend while we were there. That should keep you occupied."

I stared blankly at the manila folder sitting on the coffee table between us that contained the orders he had printed from the *Plates & Frames R Us* website. Working on them always helped make the time pass, but I wanted to take a break from them that day.

Jules rose to his feet after he received what I assumed was the text he'd been waiting for. He grabbed the folder from the table and handed it to me. "Just busy yourself with the designs, and I'll be sure to let you know what happened when I get back. Alex just got to Alora's apartment, and she's heading up to see if she's ready to go. I need to get to the restaurant and secure a booth for the three of us." He patted me on my shoulder as he walked to the door to let himself out.

"You think you guys will be out long? I may hit the beach to do some bodyboarding or something." I turned and faced the door after dropping the folder onto the couch cushion next to me.

"I'm not expecting this to be an all-day event, but when we'll leave all depends on how busy it is today, or how long we sit around to talk."

"That gives me time to enjoy the beach for myself for once."

"I'll see you when we finish eating, then. I may bring Alex with me, so be prepared for one extra guest. And be careful out there," he said as he opened the door to leave.

"Don't worry about me. I'll be fine."

Jules nodded as he closed the door behind him. I turned back around and sunk into the couch again, and then I slowly began pushing the folder to the edge of the couch so it'd eventually fall to the floor. I loved my ability to sketch amazing custom pieces for cars with coal and different color pastels. At times, though, I wanted a break from using my craft. But it was summer; orders were coming in from everywhere from people who wanted new and flashy car accessories to show off as they drove around town. I let the folder get as close to the edge as possible, only to snatch it up and leaf through its contents. The design descriptions that the customers wrote in the comments field on each order form seemed basic enough for me to put off for a little while longer, so I decided to head to the beach before working on any of them.

After slipping into my wetsuit jacket and grabbing my bodyboard and flippers, I headed down to my car. Once I was situated, I drove to the beach. There weren't many people there when I arrived; I was happy about that. I took a moment to stretch in the sand before putting on my flippers and going out into the ocean. I checked for any signs indicating that there were strong rip currents. I didn't want to drown again like I had two years earlier. There was no guarantee that if that happened a second time I would come back from it. Once I was sure that the water was safe, I waded out into the coolness of it.

I caught some decent-sized waves for what felt like the entire afternoon. When I was tired and ready to go home, I swam back to the beach and stretched again after pulling my flippers off. I found a large seashell resting close by, so I took a moment to dig into the sand beneath it. I found something that Alora had buried after scooping out only a few handfuls of sand. When I was done reading it, I refilled the hole and walked back to my car. After dusting as much sand off of me as possible before getting in, I made a quick stop at a nearby gas station to grab some snacks and then headed home.

Once I got back, I placed the new piece of writing into the wooden box with the others and jumped in the shower to wash the leftover sand off of myself and my wetsuit jacket. After I hung it to dry, I threw on a pair of khaki cargo shorts and an old T-shirt, grabbed the folder from the couch, and then sat down at the dining room table so I could start working on some of the designs. Halfway through one of the sketches, though, I ended up falling asleep at the table when I put my head down to rest my eyes for what I thought would be a brief moment.

I jumped up from my nap when my phone vibrated loudly on the table. I looked down at the sketch I was working on and saw that the design was smeared from my falling asleep on it. I stretched in the chair as I checked my phone, noticing that I had a voice mail from Jules. I listened to the message, which was straight and to the point: he wanted me to call him back as soon as I got it. I didn't hesitate to hit the redial button. The phone rang twice before he picked up.

"James?" Jules whispered.

"I'm sure that's what the caller ID said," I said sarcastically. "Why do you sound like you're in trouble?" I whispered back.

"Why're you whispering?"

"Because *you're* whispering," I hissed. "What's going on? What's so urgent that you needed me to call you back when you're in the middle of lunch with Alex and Alora?"

"Hang on."

I heard him take the phone away from his ear. Clicking sounds on his end told me that he was responding to a text message. When he came back, he sounded like he was trying to cover something up.

"Nothing. How was the beach?" He was no longer whispering.

"It was fine. That's not why you called me, Jules. You could have asked me *that* when you swung by later."

"I meant to call someone else?" He was obviously trying to cover something up.

"Who? Matt?"

"Yes! That's who I meant to call. I wanted to ask him—"

"How the camping trip with him, his parents, and Samantha is going? I know you wouldn't call them while they're on vacation unless there was something important you wanted to talk about. And I'd hope you'd talk to *me* about it before him. So I'll ask you one more time: what's going on?" I grew even more suspicious when I heard him take the phone away from his ear and start to text again. At that point, I was frustrated and ready to hang up. I waited until he put the phone back to his ear before speaking again. "Listen, if you don't have anything to tell me, I'd like to get back to my sketching. These designs aren't going to create themselves," I puffed.

"How far have you gotten with them, anyway?"

"Pretty far; I'm almost finished. I just have a few more and they'll all be done."

"Okay, well, I'll be by later, so I'll talk to you then, okay?"

"Okay?" I answered, confused.

Without saying another word, he hung up. I shook my head as I stared at my phone and then placed it back on the table. "He's gone crazy," I mumbled as I grabbed a piece of bright yellow pastel and worked to fix the smears on the paper. It didn't take long to correct it and start on the next design. Before I knew it, the conversation wasn't even on my mind anymore because I was so focused on what was in front of me.

—Chapter 6—

I was working on the next-to-last design that was in the folder when knocking on the front door broke my concentration. I answered the door, and Jules didn't hesitate to walk past me and have a seat at the dining room table without saying a word. He gathered all of the finished designs that were in clear page protectors as he waited for me to sit back down.

"Hello to you, too." After closing the door, I flopped into the seat I had originally been in and continued working.

"These are amazing, James." Jules held one up so he could take a good look at it.

"Uh-huh." I grabbed a dark shade of blue pastel to mix in with a lighter shade of blue that I had been using before he arrived. "Is Alex coming?"

"Yeah, she should be here in a few minutes. She's driving Alora home."

"Okay."

We both fell silent as I began sketching again. Once I was finished with the design, I put it in an unoccupied page protector and placed it in the pile with the others. I figured I'd save the last one so I'd have something to do the next day. Jules occupied himself by poking through some of the pastels that were spread all over the table on paper towels. Light knocking at the door prompted him to get up and answer it as I started to put the pastels away in the small box they belonged in.

"Hey," I heard him say after he opened the door.

"Hey yourself," I heard Alex reply.

She came in and sat at the opposite end of the table. Jules closed the door, locked it, and then came back over to the table and took a seat. They both sat and watched me put away all of my art materials. When I was finished, I looked up at the both of them. "You two are awful quiet. What—no news report today about your lunch date?"

"You didn't tell him?" Alex asked.

"I figured I'd wait until you got here. I didn't want to jump the gun and say anything in case things changed while you were driving her home," Jules explained.

I raised an eyebrow suspiciously. "Tell me what?"

"It's about Alora and Jordan," Alex began. "Alora got a call from him while we were waiting to place our order. Long story short, he dumped her."

I narrowed my eyes as I processed what she had just told me. "You're lying."

"What? No! I'm being serious!" she proclaimed. "I found her in the bathroom on the verge of a meltdown. She told me that's why he called. He said he didn't think they should see each other anymore. I *swear* I'm telling the truth. This isn't something I'd lie to you about."

I stared at her for a few more seconds and then looked to Jules. He raised his hands in a gesture of defense. "I honestly didn't notice anything until I realized Alex wasn't responding to me while I was talking to her. I could tell by the look on *her* face that something was wrong with Alora. It was like Alex's facial expression matched what Alora was feeling. Maybe her gift is having a heightened sense of empathy?"

"I don't think that's considered a special gift," I objected.

"Why?" Jules challenged. "I can't see why that couldn't be something she acquired when she came back."

"Maybe . . ."

I thought about what he said and reevaluated my opinion about it. The three of us had come back to the world of the living with something extra. I was able to tell if someone had passed on and come back or had a near-death experience. For a while, Jules was able to go between worlds and travel while he dreamed, as well as sense when Alex was in trouble. But because he went to help her through her near-death experience so she wouldn't completely cross over, he was stripped of the former and left with the latter. As for Alex—we weren't sure what special gift she had come back with. It was still touch and go.

"You'll let us know when you think you're experiencing something out of the norm, right?" I asked her. "That's the only way we'll be able to help you hone in on it, and maybe work on making it useful."

"If I'm able to at the time, yes," Alex promised.

I continued the conversation at hand. "I'm sorry I accused you of lying. I'm really not sure how to feel about this right now," I admitted.

"I expected you to do back flips around your apartment or try and visit her at her place with a dozen roses," Jules laughed.

"Did she say why he was the one to break it off? I half-expected for her to do it herself."

"She was upset that he beat her to the punch, but she didn't say anything about his reasoning behind it. I'm sure he just wanted the upper hand, as usual." Alex got up, went into the kitchen, and grabbed three bottles of water from the fridge. She handed them out to us as she sat back down. She winced as she tried to get comfortable.

"Did you want to lay on the couch so you can stretch out your leg?" I offered as I opened my water.

"If that's okay with you." She slowly got back up from the chair.

"Of course. In fact, we'll come and sit over there with you. There's no point in being uncomfortable if you need to rest your leg."

The three of us got up and went over to the couch in the front room. Alex stretched out and rested her left leg on Jules's lap. I sat across from them in the loveseat.

"So what's next?" she asked as she sank into the soft couch cushion.

"That's up to James." Jules looked to me and waited for an answer.

"I honestly don't know what's next. I've been waiting all this time to actually get the ball rolling with her, and now all of the sudden I'm at a loss for words. I thought we'd have some kind of warning for when this would happen. When do you think I should say something to her?"

"Personally, I think you should approach her as soon as you can. We'll be on campus enrolling for our fall classes while you're in class tomorrow, so maybe you can randomly appear when you get out and we'll introduce you to her. That'll break the ice," Alex suggested.

"That seems *extremely* cliché," I pointed out.

"I'm not sure what else to suggest then, James," Alex said. "She'll probably be hanging around us most of the time now. But I'm telling you right now, if you don't say anything to her by some time tomorrow at least, there's no telling if someone else will beat you to it. For all you know, Jordan may sweet talk his way back in. I know that's not something you want to hear, but it could happen. I wouldn't put it past him." She took a sip of her water and set the bottle on the carpet.

"Do you think that could happen, Jules? Jordan talking his way back in, I mean."

"From what I've experienced in the couple of run-ins I've had with him, he's very manipulative. If he wants something, I'm willing to bet he'll go to great lengths to get it. Especially if he finds out someone is already considering taking his place."

He made a valid point. Rumor had it that Jordan had a way with words. If he *really* wanted to convince Alora that he was sorry and wanted her back, he probably could with that silver tongue of his.

Alex took her phone out of her pocket when we all heard it vibrate. Her face went blank as she read the screen. "I can't believe this," she gasped.

"Is everything okay?" I asked.

She handed Jules her phone so he could read what she read. He frowned when he was finished and handed it back to her. "How's she supposed to get by without any money?" he shouted.

I groaned in aggravation. "What's going on? Stop talking as if I'm not right here."

"Sorry." Alex tossed me her phone without warning. I caught it in midair and read the text. It was from Alora. Apparently, she had some money stashed away that was supposed to tide her over so she could pay rent until she found a job. But Jordan went by her place while they were out to eat and took all the cash out of her car after returning the spare keys to it and her apartment. She was heading to the beach to try and clear her head.

"This has to be a joke." I tossed the phone back to Jules. He caught it and then handed it back to Alex. "He would seriously do something like that?"

"It doesn't surprise me, especially if he had some idea that she was squirreling away the money he was giving her," Alex said. "Hey! You should go to the beach and just so happen to bump into her."

I instantly got nervous. "I don't think I can do it tonight."

"You were *just* getting on to me this morning about how we're always reporting how she's doing and how you're never able to do anything. Now you can take some sort of action and you don't think you can 'randomly' bump into her?" Jules tossed one of the couch throw pillows across the room, and it hit me in the face.

"C'mon, she'll be there with Raven. You should *seriously* go," Alex pressed.

"Can't I just wait until tomorrow and do what you suggested to begin with?" I pleaded as I dropped the pillow on the floor by my feet.

"No," they answered simultaneously.

Jules helped Alex up from the couch and grabbed both of their bottles of water. She did a couple of stretches that her physical therapist taught her for when her leg got stiff and then they walked to the front door to leave. I followed them.

"Don't wait too late to head over there; if you approach her when it's dark out, you might scare her." Alex hugged me and walked out into the breezeway. "And before you go, you'll want to wash the pastel off of your cheek," she giggled.

I rubbed my hand on the left side of my face and saw two different shades of blue on it from when I had fallen asleep on the design I was working on. I rubbed my hands together, embarrassed. "Thanks for pointing that out."

"Call me if you need anything. We'll be at my place watching a few movies and going over the classes we're enrolling in tomorrow." Jules stepped out into the breezeway as well and watched Alex as she slowly made her way down the stairs to his apartment.

"Can't you two come with me?" I whispered as I grabbed his arm just before he started to walk away. I was desperate to have someone come along so I wasn't alone when I approached her for the first time.

"I didn't have someone come with me when I met Alex for the first time. Use the same advice you gave me: don't think too much into it. It'll work out for the best. You'll be fine."

Jules gave my shoulder a squeeze and headed downstairs to let Alex into his apartment. I closed the door and looked at the time. It was starting to get late; I had a few minutes to clean myself up before it started to get dark out. I quickly washed my face and hands, and kicked on a pair of sneakers while pulling on my favorite hoodie over my T-shirt. I was on my way out the door when I thought of something that would help to break the ice when I approached Alora. I quickly backtracked to the dining room table, and grabbed one of my mini sketch pads, my pencil set, pastel box, and a few small page protectors; one of them having black lining. *I can sketch a picture of her and give it to her as a gift,* I thought. *It can be a conversation starter. Hopefully this works . . .*

—Chapter 7—

When I arrived at the beach, I didn't see Alora's car in the parking lot. I was glad she hadn't arrived yet. It gave me time to sit and work up the courage to approach her when she got there. I walked up the steps to the wooden deck so I could sit down on one of the wooden benches that looked out to the ocean. The sky was starting to change colors as the sun prepared to set. To pass the time until she got there, I started to sketch the sight before me. I even included some of the small bonfires that were being set up by a few groups of people waiting for it to get dark enough to light them. Before I knew it, I had sketched three different pictures and placed them in separate page protectors for safekeeping. I admired my work as I stood up and took a long stretch, and then I began to put my coal pencils and pastels away. My phone rang as I was cleaning up around myself. It was Jules.

"Yeah," I answered as I closed the pastel box.

"Have you talked to her yet?"

I looked back at the parking lot and saw her car parked three or four cars away from mine at the end of the row. I hadn't even realized that she had arrived. I was so into my sketching that I hadn't bothered checking periodically for her. "Um . . . not yet. I'm working on it, though."

"You didn't see her pull up, did you?" Jules laughed.

"It's not funny."

"I know, I know. That's why I called. Alora confirmed with Alex that she got to the beach safely and that she'd be there for a while. I just wanted to make sure *you* knew she was there."

"Thanks for the heads up," I sighed.

"No problem. Good luck."

I hung up with him and scanned the beach as I shoved the phone into my hoodie pocket. For a second, I couldn't find her. But then I saw her playing with a puppy, who I assumed was Raven, a few feet away from where I was sitting. She was staying away from the bonfires that other beachgoers were building so they wouldn't disturb anyone. Her sundress was flowing in the breeze as she tossed a stick into the water for Raven to fetch. When the puppy brought it back to her, she tossed it again. I gathered my things and walked down to one of the bonfires further away. The people who built it were sitting around it and quietly talking to one another. I recognized them; it was a small group of guys I had gone to high school with and whom I saw occasionally on campus.

"Hey, guys," I greeted them.

"Oh, hey, James. What's up?" one of them said. He scooted over so I could sit between him and another person.

I plopped down on the cold log and opened my sketch pad. "You mind if I sit here and sketch something? I promise I won't get in your way or jump into your conversation."

"Sure, sure, anything you want to do man. Hey, how're your parents?"

"They're doing fine. Thanks for asking. How are you? How are *all* of you?"

They all confirmed that they were doing well and to tell my folks they said hello. I promised I would as I began working. First, I sketched the unlit pile of wood for the bonfire in front of me. Then I did it again, only the second time, I included everyone sitting around it, excluding myself. I ripped it out of the book and handed to the guy sitting to my right.

"You were always good with this sort of thing, James," he said as he passed it around the circle so everyone could look at it. "You still working at *Plates & Frames R Us?*"

"Yup, going on two years now." I took the sketch back when it got back around to me, initialed it at the bottom, and handed it to the guy to my right again. "It's yours—no charge." I said with a smile.

"Thanks. You about to work on another one?"

"Before it gets too dark, yes."

"You've only got a few minutes, so you may want to hurry. We're about to light the bonfire, and I don't think the heat from this sucker will agree with your pastels since we're so close to it."

He was right. So as I watched Alora continue to play with Raven in the distance, I quickly began to sketch what I could while there were still brilliant colors in the sky. The guy next to me looked on while the others talked amongst themselves and readied some marshmallows and graham crackers. Moments later, I was finished. I quickly initialed the bottom and rubbed my fingers over some of the colors to get them to smear together better.

"I'm sure she'll like it," the guy said, giving me a thumbs-up as he got ready to light the bonfire.

"Thanks. I'll catch you guys later. It was good seeing you."

I got up and walked away from them as the sun finally set. Apparently, Alora was also getting ready to leave. After tossing the stick off to the side, she scratched Raven between the ears, picked her up, and headed back to the parking lot. I stopped and waited briefly as the sky began to fill with stars. I heard the bonfires roar behind me one by one as a cool ocean breeze blew sand into the air, which caused me to pull my hood over my head. I looked inside the sketch pad again at the picture I had drawn of her and rubbed on some of the colors again to make sure it looked perfect.

Here goes nothing, I thought as I took a deep breath.

I made my way down the same sandy path she took and saw her instructing Raven to sit as she beat the sand off of the bottom of her sandals, and then she dried Raven off with a small towel. She then opened her trunk and grabbed what looked to be a couple of dog treats after tossing the towel inside of it. She placed them on the ground and checked her phone for messages as the puppy took her time eating. I figured that was my chance to make my move, so I began a light jog toward her. The closer I got, the more it felt like my heart was going to beat out of my chest.

I slowed to a walk when I heard Raven begin to growl. Alora looked up from her phone and saw me approaching. She sat her phone on the ground, scooped Raven up into her arms, and quickly got into the car. She sat her on the passenger seat and locked all the car doors before I could even touch the concrete. By the time I got to her, she had started the car. She was in so much of a hurry to get away from what she thought was a threat that she left her phone on the ground. I picked it up when I got to her car, lightly knocked on the window, and waited for her to hopefully give me a moment of her time before she headed back home.

—Chapter 8—

On the way to the beach, I made a quick stop at the diner that Alex works at to see if they had any job openings. I told the manager who I was, and he told me to come back the next day with Alex for an interview. It was something, so it made me feel a little better about my current situation.

When I arrived, I saw that other beachgoers were there setting up bonfires for when the sun set. I walked Raven a good distance away from them so her running and barking while playing wouldn't interrupt them. I found a decent-sized stick in the sand and began tossing it around. I took it back from her when she brought it to me and then tossed it again. She was enjoying herself, which made me happy that I had taken her there. She deserved it.

When it started to get dark, the temperature dropped a little, so I figured it was time to leave. The groups scattered on the beach were preparing to light their bonfires as the sun finally set for the night. I picked Raven up after tossing the stick away and scratched between her ears as I made my way to the sandy path we had taken to get onto the beach itself. I could tell that Raven was exhausted from all the running around she had done, so I knew she'd get a good night's sleep.

After we got back to the car, I instructed her to sit as I beat the sand off of the bottom of my sandals. When I was finished, I grabbed a raggedy towel from the back seat and dried her off with it. She sat still as I dried her paws and fur as best I could. I opened the trunk, tossed the damp towel into it, and grabbed a few of her treats, and I placed them down on the ground for her as I started to check my phone for any messages. When I saw I didn't have any, I started to compose a text to Alex to let her know that I had gone by her job to see if they had any openings and about the interview the next day.

Just as I was about to hit the send button, I heard Raven emit a low growl. I looked up from my phone and saw someone walking toward us from the sandy path that we had just taken to get back to the car. Not sure who it was because it was already too dark to recognize anyone, I scooped Raven up and quickly sat her in the passenger seat of the car and then got in myself. I locked the doors and tried not to panic. Raven whined and paced nervously in the passenger seat, and then she suddenly began barking wildly at the driver-side window. I looked over and saw the stranger getting closer to the car. "Good girl, Raven. That's a good girl," I praised her as I patted her between her ears. I then grabbed my car keys and started the car so I could speed off into the night. For a second she grew quiet, but then she began barking wildly again when the stranger lightly knocked on the window. He patiently waited for me to acknowledge him, but I stared blankly ahead of me and didn't respond as Raven's barks and growls grew louder and louder.

"Miss," I heard him say through the glass.

I still didn't say anything, hoping that if I didn't, he'd go away. I was trying to figure out if I had anything in the car to fight him off with if it came to that. I realized I had nothing. The stranger knocked on the window lightly again as he peered in at both me and Raven. I cleared my throat and signaled for her to stop barking. She sat back and got quiet. "Please get away from my car, or I'll call the police!" I shouted. I reached into the cup holder that I usually sat my phone in when I got into the car and noticed that it wasn't there. The stranger knocked on my window a third time, but I didn't pay him any attention as I frantically looked for it. "I mean it! Go away! I'll call them without hesitation!" I shouted again. I felt around the passenger seat but still couldn't find it. "Dammit . . ." I checked the back seat where I had grabbed the towel to dry Raven off in hopes that it'd be there. I punched the back seat when I didn't find it back there, either. When the stranger knocked on the window a fourth time, I looked up to find my phone pressed against it in the palm of his hand. My eyes widened when I realized I had left it on the ground after I had picked Raven up to put her in the car. "Just leave it where you found it and walk away from the car! I'll get it myself!"

The stranger held his hand up to his ear to show that he couldn't hear me. When I shouted to him again, he put his hand up to his ear again. *What's he up to?* I thought as he gestured for me to roll down my window. I reached into my purse, grabbed a pen, and secured it between my index and middle finger in case I had to poke him in the eye with it. I figured cracking the window a little bit was safer than opening the car door. I rolled down the window enough to be able to feel the ocean breeze blow in and hear what the stranger was saying.

"You can't call the police on anyone without your phone," he laughed.

Whoever he was, he didn't sound like a threat, but his hood was shadowing his entire face. I didn't want to take any chances, so I stayed in the car. "I thought you couldn't hear me?" I sneered.

He shrugged.

"I have a backup phone," I threatened.

"I highly doubt that."

We stared each other down through the window and didn't speak as we waited for the other to say something.

"Well? Do you want your phone back or not?" he asked.

"Of course I want my phone back. It's *my* phone."

"You're pretty snippy for someone who doesn't have something they're so frantic to recover. I'm just trying to be a Good Samaritan. I'm not here to hurt you, or your puppy."

"How do *I* know that? You could be a maniac hermit that snatches up women from the beach at night and holds them hostage in your hermit tent."

I realized that I had let my imagination get the best of me. I heard the stranger laugh and shuffle what he was carrying under his arm.

"That's quite a wild allegation if I've ever heard one. Tell you what—how about I just slip the phone to you through the window. I'll need you to roll it down some more since I don't think it'll fit through this nothing of a crack you've already made. Don't worry. I won't use my hermit teeth to rip your fingers off if they get too close to my face," he joked.

I snickered as I let the window down a little more and watched as he slipped the phone in to me slowly. When he let it go, I caught it before it landed in my lap and then rolled the window back up, leaving a smaller crack in it than there was to begin with. I wanted to call Alex or Jules right then and there to tell them I thought I was in danger, but when I saw the stranger smiling at me through the window, I didn't feel as frightened as I had when I first saw him approaching the car. Raven slowly climbed onto my lap and pressed her nose against the window to get a better look at him. He wiggled his index finger at her, which caused her to wag her tail in excitement.

"She's cute," he complimented.

"She's more vicious than she is cute, trust me," I falsely claimed.

"I'm sure she is," he chuckled.

When I realized I had spent too much time talking to a complete stranger just to get my phone back, I put the car in gear so I could leave. "Thanks for returning my phone," I said as I went to roll up the window.

"Wait, I have something for you."

I watched as he pulled what looked to be a small sketch pad from under his arm. He quickly opened it, ripped out one of the pages, shoved it into what looked to be a small sheet of black plastic, and slipped it through the crack of the window. The corner of it poked me in the cheek before it landed daintily on my lap. "Are you trying to poke my eye out?" I cried. I flipped down the overhead mirror and checked to make sure it hadn't broken the skin.

"I'm sorry. I didn't mean for that to happen." He took a step back from the window with his hands up to show he hadn't meant any harm.

I snatched what he had given me off of my lap and dropped it between the front seats. Without saying another word to him, I drove off into the night. When I looked in my rearview mirror, I saw him watching as I drove away. "What a weirdo, huh, Raven?"

—Chapter 9—

"Wait, I have something for you."

Alora watched as I pulled my sketch pad from under my arm. I quickly opened it, ripped out the sketch of her, shoved it into the only page protector with the black lining I had brought with me, and slipped it to her through the crack in the window before she could roll it up. The corner of it poked her in the cheek before it landed daintily on her lap. "Are you trying to poke my eye out?" She flipped down the overhead mirror and checked to make sure it hadn't broken the skin.

I apologized and took a step back from the window with my hands up, showing I hadn't meant any harm.

She moved the drawing off of her lap and dropped it between the front seats. Without saying another word to me, she drove off into the night. I stood in silence as I watched her drive away.

I slowly walked up to the second floor of the building I stayed in. I wasn't looking forward to the talk I was about to have with Alex and Jules. I hoped that I got there before Alora called and told them what had happened so I could get a word in edgewise. I knocked on Jules's apartment door and waited only a few seconds before Alex let me in. They were watching TV in the front room. I dropped my sketch pad and drawing tools on the floor as I flopped into the armchair that was across from the couch.

"So how'd it go?" Alex sat next to Jules and waited for the scoop. Jules cut off the TV so he wouldn't be distracted.

"Uh . . . well, I kind of waited a little late to approach her, and—"

"*Please* tell me you at least approached her with*out* that hood over your head," Jules said flatly.

I stared at the both of them blankly and shook my head as I pulled my hood down.

Jules squeezed the bridge of his nose and sighed exasperatedly. "James, we *told* you to go up to her while she could tell you weren't some creepy beach hermit."

I groaned. "What's the deal with you people and beach hermits? Are those even real?" I remembered that that's what Alora had accused me of being when she asked for her phone back.

"It's nothing we can't straighten out for him tomorrow, Jules. Don't be so hard on him." Alex nudged him lightly.

He rolled his eyes. "James was hard on me when it was the other way around. And who wears a hoodie to the beach, anyway?"

"You and James are two completely different people. I'm sure tonight wasn't a total loss. I haven't heard from Alora yet, so maybe she wasn't all that freaked out. And it gets chilly out there when the sun sets, no matter what time of the year it is. You know that."

"Oh, I'm sure you'll hear from her. Just give her time to get home and settle in for the night," Jules said.

"Can you two *please* stop talking about my situation as if I'm not sitting right across from you?" I shouted.

They both looked at me like two deer caught in headlights.

"We're sorry, James," Alex apologized. "We're so used to discussing this amongst ourselves that we sometimes forget that you're the big piece in all this. What did you have to say?"

"What can he possibly say? He'll be lucky if he can come back from what happened tonight," Jules huffed.

"Do you want to talk to him alone then?" Alex asked. "I should head home anyway. It's getting late."

"I'll walk you down to your car," he offered.

"I can get down there just fine on my own. Don't worry about me. I'll see you guys tomorrow."

Alex grabbed her purse and left without saying another word. When she was gone, I tried to tell Jules what had happened. He wasn't hearing it though; he thought I was making up excuses. "What's *so* hard about walking up to her and just saying, 'Hi, how are you? My name is—' and going from there?"

"You know, if I remember correctly, you were nervous the day before you approached Alex. I wasn't getting on you about it then," I pointed out.

"You did the night she got on that ship at the restaurant and hurt herself," Jules corrected.

"That was something altogether different. She could have gotten herself killed; you *needed* to be told about yourself."

We sat in silence briefly and stared at the coffee table between us.

"Okay, I'm confused. You've been waiting so long to step in and take Jordan's place when the time was right, but the second it's go time, you turn into a coward." Jules scooted to the edge of the couch and rested his elbows on his knees.

"*Coward* is a strong word," I mumbled.

"At this point, I couldn't care less if it's the *wrong* word. You're not trying to sabotage this, are you?"

I snickered. "Why would I do that?"

"I don't know, James. Why would you approach a female who's alone with a puppy, in the dark, at the beach, while wearing something that practically shadows your entire face?"

"Look, can what I did be corrected or not?" I puffed.

"Of course it can, especially if Alex doesn't hear from Alora tonight. If you're lucky, she'll go home and try to forget the whole thing even happened."

"Okay, then."

Jules laughed and rubbed his forehead lightly. "I just want to help you, James. In order for me or Alex to be able to do that, you've got to drop this newfound coy act to*night*." We both got to our feet after I picked up my drawing materials. I walked to the front door so I could head up to my apartment for the night, and Jules followed. "Why do you have your pencils and stuff?" he asked as he opened the door for me.

"If things can be corrected like you said, you'll find out why tomorrow. Right now, I just want to go to bed and try to pretend like the whole thing didn't happen, too."

"Right . . . well, we'll see you tomorrow then. I'll text you if I hear anything before you get out of class."

We nodded to each other, and I went up the last flight of stairs to my apartment. I walked in and quietly closed the door behind me. I dropped my stuff on the table and walked to my bedroom as I cut off all the lights on the way. After changing out of the clothes I had worn to the beach, I fell on the bed face down. The overwhelming feelings of stupidity and embarrassment were still swirling in my stomach. I knew what I *should* have done, but I was so busy trying to do things differently that I could have possibly ruined things with Alora. But knowing Alex and Jules, they'd do everything they could to set things straight the next day. I worked to try and push what had happened at the beach out of my mind as I slowly drifted off to sleep.

—Chapter 10—

I walked sluggishly into my art appreciation class the next morning and took a seat in the middle of the room. While waiting for the professor to arrive, I worked on a couple of the sketches I had done the night before at the beach. Other students walked in and glanced at my work; a few of them whispered and pointed as they took their seats. Two girls lingered for a minute before I realized I was being watched.

"I really like this one." One of them ran her finger over the pink and orange shading from the sunset I had sketched while sitting at the unlit bonfire. "Do you give lessons on how to use coals and pastels?" she inquired.

I looked up at them; they were both smiling at me.

"No."

I pulled the sketch closer to me and went back to what I was doing. They both snickered and walked to the back of the room. I checked my phone to see if I had gotten anything from either Alex or Jules, but there was still no word from them. *They should be finished with the counselor by now*, I thought. *What's taking them so long to tell me if Alora said anything to them about last night?* I shoved the phone into my pocket when the professor walked in and focused on her lecture for the day.

After class, I walked out to the courtyard. I found Jules sitting at one of the tables by himself. That wasn't normal since Alex was usually by his side as if they were connected by an invisible bungee cord. *I hope nothing's wrong.* He didn't look upset, so there had to be a reason he was alone that morning. "Where's Alex? It's rare to find you two apart unless she's at work, in a different class than you, or at home."

"She's with Alora. Apparently she stopped by the diner she works at last night and has an interview there today. They both went up there this morning together to see if she could get a waitressing job."

"How'd our counselor take that?"

"She wasn't too thrilled to handle Alora's class registration since she's not *her* counselor, but she made a one-time exception. I explained the situation to her, and she seemed to understand. She wasn't happy about not being able to talk to Alex about the classes she wanted to register for either, but she let that slide, too. She looked a little pale; that's probably why she didn't put up much of a fight. I hope she's feeling okay."

"We should really get her a fruit basket or something," I said. "She's been extremely patient with the three of us since Alex's accident."

"I was just telling Alex that last night. If it weren't for her, she'd still be ridiculously far behind when it comes to her credits." Jules slid off of the table so we could walk to our cars.

We ended up in Jordan's path on the way to the parking lot; he was leaving the same one we were heading toward. We continued talking to each other and tried to ignore the fact that he was getting closer. He was eyeing Jules mischievously and didn't look like he would make an attempt to move to the side as we approached. We split apart from each other to let him walk between us, but instead, he bumped into Jules to push him farther to the side of the sidewalk.

"Oops," Jordan laughed as he kept walking.

Jules stopped dead in his tracks and watched as Jordan disappeared around one of the nearby buildings. He closed his eyes, took a deep breath, and nodded in the direction we were originally heading to signal that he was ready to start walking again.

"I don't know why you don't lay him out." I pulled out my car fob and popped the trunk. "I'm sure it'd only take three seconds flat. I bet he's got a glass jaw."

"I'm not worried about it. He'll get what's coming to him sooner or later. I won't be the one to dish out whatever it is, though."

I carefully placed my art materials into the leather bag my parents had bought me. They supported my craft so much that they always did whatever they could to make sure I had the best supplies they could find. I partially thought that they had been going overboard ever since I came out of the coma I went into after drowning, but I was grateful that they were supportive, regardless. Their most recent gift of custom-sized page protectors was helpful when it came to protecting anything I sketched from smudging.

"So how's the art class going? Not that you need it or anything." Jules watched as I closed the trunk of my car.

"It's a dumb elective to some, but I need it to fulfill my course requirements. Plus it's the last class I have to take to catch up with you guys for our junior year."

"You know what I meant by that."

Jules hopped up and sat on the trunk of my car. I sighed and did the same. "It's going fine. I may not 'need' it, but I'm learning a few extra tricks. If anything, it's helping me get better."

"I'll say," Jules agreed. "I'm thinking you should talk to the boss about upping the prices for the work you do at the market. We'll make a bigger profit."

"I've thought about it. Maybe I'll bring it up this weekend. I've got bigger things to worry about right now, like this final project that's due at the end of this summer session."

"And what happened last night?"

"Yeah." I looked to the ground, still embarrassed about how things had unfolded at the beach.

"You put too much thought into it. I guess I can't blame you. You knew her situation would change at some point; you just didn't know when. Maybe we should have prepared you or something."

"Maybe . . . it probably wouldn't have made a difference, though."

I stared off into the distance as Jules took a call. I could hear Alex talking frantically, but it didn't sound like anything was wrong. Every time he tried to say something, she cut him off. After a minute or two of not saying anything so she could get it all out, he agreed to something she asked and then told her a time. He exhaled loudly through his mouth after he hung up the phone.

"What's going on now?" A part of me didn't want to ask out of fear that it was something I didn't want to hear.

"You got any plans for the rest of the day?" he asked me.

"Why?"

"Apparently Alora got the job and she's starting today. Alex wants you to come by so you can be properly introduced to her."

"Ugh . . ." I rubbed my forehead. "You're going with me, right?"

"Yeah, we'll head over there for their lunch break. That'll be in about two hours."

I looked at my phone and saw that that'd give me time to work on the last sketch for work that needed to be finished by the end of the week and catch a quick nap. "Did Alora say anything to Alex about her trip to the beach last night?"

"Not to my knowledge. Maybe she didn't think much of it seeing as how nothing happened to her."

My stomach sank. I had worked hard on that sketch of her and Raven at the beach. Obviously what I had slipped to her didn't pique her curiosity enough, whether she was able to see what the drawing was of right off the bat or not.

"I've got some errands to run before heading home." Jules slid off of the trunk and landed softly on his feet. "I'll pick you up when I'm finished. Be ready when I get there so we'll have time to work out a game plan before we go into the diner." He got in his car and left me in the parking lot. I took my time driving home, trying to think of things to say to Alora when we arrived.

—Chapter 11—

"Thanks again for coming with me to the interview." I struggled to tie the back of the apron that was given to me after I was told I was hired. It still smelled of fresh fabric as if it had just been made the day before. I watched as Alex put hers on as well and then washed her hands. She then came over to me and helped me tie my apron.

"Don't mention it. This is an amazing fresh start for you, so hopefully you'll have enough for rent in a few weeks."

"I hope so," I sighed after she finished helping me.

"If you need help, you know you can ask me and I'll do what I can. So how was the beach last night?"

I thought about the guy who had approached my car when I was heading home. I had been scared at first, granted, but I knew I could sometimes be overdramatic. For all I knew, he was on his way to his car and noticed I left my phone on the ground when I saw him. So in all reality, I felt foolish. "I just played fetch with Raven for a bit and then headed home. There were a few groups of people out there building their usual bonfires to light once it was dark enough, so it was my typical run-of-the-mill visit."

"Oh . . . okay, then." Alex shrugged and led me out to the front of the diner behind the front counter. She showed me where all the coffee mugs, plates, bowls, and silverware were. Afterward, she introduced me to everyone who worked with us. A few minutes later, she disappeared into the back so she could call Jules and tell him the good news. It was slow that morning, so I felt comfortable standing behind the counter until she got back. A man who looked to be in his mid-thirties came in and sat on one of the stools across from me. He looked around for a few seconds before letting me know that he wanted to order something.

"What can I get you, sir?"

"Coffee, please," he requested.

"Coming right up."

I turned my back to him and quickly prepared his beverage in a crisp white mug. After placing two creamers and some packs of sugar on the paper place mat with a spoon, I sat the mug in front of him so he could add the condiments to his liking.

"Thank you." He took a sip and placed it on the counter. "This is very good."

"You're welcome." I wiped my hands with a dishcloth that was close by.

"Could you possibly direct me to the nearby college campus? I'm a bit turned around."

"Oh, sure." I gave him the directions he needed, and we held a minute or two of small talk with each other. We didn't get a chance to exchange names, but I didn't think that mattered. Before leaving, he shook my hand and ended up holding it for an extended period of time as he looked deep into my eyes.

"Thank you again for the directions," he said with a smile.

I smiled back nervously as he continued to hold my hand. "Not a problem." It was almost as though he was waiting for something out of the ordinary to happen, so it started to get awkward. When he saw Alex approaching, he quickly exited the diner. I opened my hand when I realized he had left something in it and found a crisp fifty dollar bill. Alex didn't see him as he walked out the door because she was looking down at her phone before putting it away in one of her apron pockets.

"Everything okay out here? Did you get any customers?"

I held up the bill I was given and stared at her.

"So is someone paying for their meal, or—"

"A man came in for a cup of coffee. I'm sure it doesn't cost *this* much, though." I turned the bill slowly and examined it.

Alex got on her tippy toes and peeked out of the diner windows. "Is he still here? Maybe he didn't mean to give you that much."

I looked outside with her and didn't see the man out there. "It looks like he's already gone. What do I do with the change?"

"Well, he paid for the coffee, that's for sure. The rest is—well—your tip. Lucky you. That's a nice one for your first day." She took the bill from me and walked over to the register. I watched as she showed me how to ring up his order. She then gave me the change.

"I don't feel right taking this. Something was weird about that guy." I tried to give it back to her, but she pushed my hand back toward me.

"It's okay. We get people like that sometimes. Now if they get *too* weird, the manager will straighten it out. If not him, then Butch will handle it, right, Butch?"

We looked through the ordering window into the kitchen at the large chef manning the stove. He smiled and nodded in agreement. *I wouldn't want to get on his bad side,* I thought.

"Jules will be stopping by later when we break for lunch," she informed me as she led me over to a table to check on the customers sitting there. She introduced me to them as a new waitress in training and then asked if everything was okay with their food. They said everything was fine, so we moved on to the next table to start wiping it down. She handed me the rubber bin so she could put the dirty dishes and utensils in it as she cleaned the table.

"Alex, I don't want visitors on my first day," I said as I followed her to the next table. "Can't it wait a few days?"

"He just wants to swing by and congratulate you, that's all. We'll enjoy a little food and then he'll leave. No biggie. Besides, the customers who come in are technically visitors too, you know." She laughed when I dropped my head back and groaned. "It'll be fine, I promise. You act like he's going to poke fun at you or something."

"I know he won't do that." I followed her to the next table that needed cleaning. "I just don't want to be distracted while I'm learning the job, that's all."

"We'll be on our lunch break, remember?" She gave me a side-glance as she set new paper place mats down.

"Right . . ."

"Alora, it's Jules, not the president of the United States. It'll be fine, so stop making a big deal out of it."

"Fine, fine," I conceded.

Time flew by as I shadowed Alex while she worked. For the most part, I was learning the job quickly—not quickly enough to feel as though I'd be okay on my own the next time I was scheduled to work, but quickly enough to take a few orders on my own while she quietly watched. Besides the tip I made for serving one cup of coffee earlier that morning, I managed to make a few more bucks. It wasn't much, but I knew that with time and patience, I'd get the swing of it and hopefully pull in larger tips.

Our lunch break came around before I knew it. We both hung our aprons in the back room after letting another waitress know we were going to eat. We grabbed a booth in the back near a window so we could keep an eye out for Jules.

"How do you like the job so far?" Alex asked after ordering some soda from the manager.

"So far, so good. I think I'll like it here. I get to work with you, so that's a bonus in itself," I laughed.

"Perfect. I'm glad you like it. And I'm glad you got the job. Wait until the manager sees how well you balance multiple items at once. Maybe you'll get a lot of hours since you can do that and multitask pretty well."

"I'll cross that bridge when I get there."

The manager brought us our drinks and took our order. I ordered something small from the employee menu since I wasn't very hungry. It was nice to know that they offered two small free meals to the workers throughout the day. The selection was pretty decent, so it wasn't difficult to find something I liked. A familiar voice caught my attention, which caused me to turn in the booth and look toward the front doors. My heart sank when I realized it was who I thought it was. I turned back to face Alex and sank into the seat. *I hope he didn't see me.*

"What's the matter with you?" She took a sip of her drink and looked outside to see if Jules had arrived.

I clenched my teeth into an awkward smile and signaled for her to look toward the front of the diner with my eyes. She leaned out of the booth to take a look and then slowly leaned back in. "What's *he* doing here?"

I knew he was on his way over to our table when she rolled her eyes and started to slowly sip her soda through her straw so she wouldn't have to say anything to him. When he got to our table, he noticed I was sitting across from her. "Oh, I had no idea you were here."

"You know my car, Jordan, so you knew I was here."

"I guess. How are you, Alexia? You're looking better."

"I'm fine, thank you." She went back to drinking.

"That's good to hear. I just stopped in to pick up an order I placed a while ago. It should be coming out any minute now. What're you doing here anyway, Alora? Shouldn't you be looking for a job or something? You *do* know you have financial responsibilities now, right?" he asked smugly.

"For your information, she *has* a job. She works here with me. She started today." Alex pushed her soda to the center of the table and sat up straight.

"You know something, Alexia? You *always* jump into conversations that don't have anything to do with you. Do you ever mind your own business when it comes to Alora?"

"Does a bear ever *not* shit in the woods?" she retorted.

He opened his mouth to answer but then closed it when he thought about the question. I was slightly confused too, but I was almost positive the answer was no.

"You can be *so* annoying. We're trying to have lunch, so why don't you go away and leave Alora alone?" she said through narrowed eyes.

"I think it's up to her to tell me that, don't you?"

They both looked at me, and my words got caught in my throat. As much as I wanted to stand up to him, there was something about him that never allowed me to. I could stand up to him and speak my mind when he wasn't around, but even after carefully rehearsing what I wanted to say to his face, I always backed down when the time came.

"I think she's still processing all of this," Jordan laughed.

"Just go *away,* Jordan," Alex demanded. "You broke up with her, and then you went and took all the money back that you had given her. There's no reason to drag this out by hanging around. Move on. Go play in traffic or jump off of a cliff—do something, *anything,* that doesn't involve being around her, or us."

Out of anger, Jordan leaned over and knocked Alex's soda over, causing it to spill and roll across the table toward her. She tried to jump up as quickly as she could to move before her lap got wet, but she hit her bad leg on the bottom of the table in the process. She sat back down quickly, grabbed her thigh, and scooted over to the window as fast as she could. I listened as the soda spilled off the table and splattered from the seat onto the floor; the ice cubes bounced off of the seat as well and broke into pieces as they cascaded across the floor.

"Alex, are you okay?" I snatched one of the cloth napkins from around the silverware. The fork and knife clashed against the tabletop, and the spoon fell under the table. Pushing Jordan aside, I slid out of the booth and went to sit next to her as I wiped the seat off while sliding in. Her face was twisted in a way I had never seen before. I could tell she was trying to stop herself from shouting out in pain. Then, without warning, Jordan was shoved to the floor. He took a few of the chairs that were pushed under a nearby table down with him as he tried to stop himself from falling. I looked down at him and saw that he was glaring at someone. I followed his gaze and found Jules standing at the end of our table with another guy close behind him. When the stranger noticed I was staring at him, he smiled nervously. Something about that smile was strangely familiar, but I couldn't put my finger on what it was.

—Chapter 12—

"You're not going to freeze up again today, are you? I'll take you back home if you are."

Jules had just picked me up from my apartment, and we were heading to the diner for Alex and Alora's lunch break. I had managed to finish the last sketch I was working on for work and change my clothes just in time to get dragged out of the house by the collar when it was obvious I was stalling.

"I think I'll do much better since you and Alex will be there," I admitted.

"That's not how you made it seem when I came to pick you up. You were taking your sweet time tidying up and everything like you were expecting company. Don't think I didn't notice that you were stalling."

"Only a little, geez. Just because I *said* I'll do much better with you two there doesn't mean I'm not nervous."

"There's nothing to be nervous about. She doesn't bite." He pulled into the parking lot of the diner and stopped next to Alex's car.

"No, but I bet *he* does." I directed Jules's attention to the front of the diner as I watched Jordan walk up the steps to go inside.

"*Seriously?*" Jules put the car in park and snatched the emergency brake in frustration. "I wonder if he knows Alora got the job."

"He does if someone told him." I reclined the passenger seat and shut my eyes as I placed both of my hands behind my head.

"What're you doing?"

"Getting comfortable. This may take a while."

"No, we need to go in there now." Jules unbuckled his seat belt and was about to get out of the car, but he saw through the diner window that Jordan had found his way to Alex and Alora's table. He dropped his forehead onto the steering wheel and groaned. "I guess we should wait until he leaves."

"*If* he leaves," I pointed out.

"He'll leave. I don't know when, but he will."

We both sat quietly and waited, hoping that we'd see Jordan walking back to his car after a minute or two so we could go inside. Suddenly, Jules insisted that we needed to get out of the car. "Something's wrong. I can feel it."

"Are you saying that because it's taking him a while to come out or because you actually sense there's a problem?"

"Both. C'mon, let's go."

We quickly got out of the car and walked inside. Just as we walked past the seating podium, we heard a glass fall on the table. We looked in the direction it had come from and saw Alex try to jump out of her seat. She wasn't successful and fell back down with a look of anguish on her face.

"Alex, are you okay?" I heard Alora ask as she pushed Jordan aside to go sit by her. Silverware clashed on the tabletop, and we heard ice come to a stop from sliding across the tile floor.

Before I could say anything, Jules stormed up to Jordan. Just as I was about to grab his arm to slow him down, he shoved Jordan to the floor and stood over him. Jordan landed in some of the ice, causing the other pieces close by to slide farther across the diner floor. A couple of nearby chairs fell with him when he tried to stop himself from falling. I looked at both Alex and Alora as I tried to figure out what to say or do and ended up smiling nervously at Alora when I noticed that she was staring at me. It looked as though she was trying to figure out if she recognized me or not. The entire diner fell silent, and all eyes were on us. I took a step back in case Jules needed room. He eyed Jordan as he slowly got to his feet.

"You can bully me, Jordan, but I *won't* allow you to bully Alexia. She's not an option, understand?"

Jordan fixed his collared shirt and kicked a piece of ice away as he tried to laugh it off. "That was a cheap shot."

"You need to leave," Jules said nonchalantly.

Jordan looked around and realized that the customers were watching us. He seemed to be trying to figure out what to do next but came up with nothing. After giving Jules a long, hard look, he pushed between the two of us and snatched his bag of food from one of the busboys who was watching from the front of the diner. We watched as he walked to his car and sped out of the parking lot.

Alora grabbed Alex's napkin and quickly wiped the table dry. "I'll go get you another soda." Grabbing the used napkins so she could take them with her, she excused herself and walked to the front of the diner. Jules found an unused napkin at one of the empty tables and slid in next to Alex after taking the silverware out so he could use it. I sat across from them.

"You okay?" Jules gave her shoulder a gentle squeeze.

Alex was resting her head on the window with her eyes closed. "I hit the table pretty hard trying to jump up before my lap got wet. The pain will go away. I just need a minute."

"So much for not being the one to dish out what's coming to him," I joked.

"I had to do something. What he did wasn't okay." Jules dried the table off a little more. "Did any get on your lap?"

"No." Alex opened her eyes to look at the both of us. "I managed to scoot close enough to the window so none of it could get on me."

Alora came back to the table with the same busboy who had handed Jordan his food on the way out following close behind her. He had a small mop and bucket on hand. "I'll be out of your way in a second. Are you okay, Alexia?" he asked as he started to work around under the table with the musty-smelling mop to get as much soda off the floor as he could.

"I'm fine."

"I can talk to the manager to see if you can get off early today. I know your leg *has* to be killing you right now." He wrung the mop into the bucket and did a second sweep under the table to try and dry it more.

"I don't think that'll be necessary."

"I'm going to ask him anyway. That was a jerk move of that guy. Way to set him straight, Julian."

The busboy dropped the mop into the bucket and patted Jules on the shoulder as he started to clean up the ice that was scattered across the floor. When he was finished, he walked back toward the front of the diner. Alora stood at the end of the table and slid a new soda over to Alex, who put a new straw in the glass and slowly took a drink.

"Maybe you *should* call it a day. You know every time you bump that leg, it sets back your physical therapy a little, and it's out of whack for a few hours. You might as well go home and rest it," Jules coaxed.

"If the manager says that it's okay, then I'll go after lunch. You're okay with that, right, Alora? We can just pick up where we left off tomorrow when we come in."

"Yeah, sure. I don't mind at all," Alora quickly agreed.

I nudged Jules's shin under the table with my foot. He looked at me and suddenly remembered why I was there to begin with. "Oh, Alora, this is my friend James. James, this is Alora," he said.

"Nice to meet you," Alora said flatly.

"Likewise?" I was disappointed at the emptiness of her greeting.

"This is my fault," she began. "If I would have told him to leave, he wouldn't have tried to knock your drink all over you."

"What did I tell you about apologizing for the things he does?" Alex took another sip of soda and strained to sit up straight.

"Admit it, Alex. If *I* had said I wanted him to leave instead of freezing up, he probably would have left. That, or he would have tried to get the soda to spill on me, not you. I can't keep allowing you to fight my battles for me."

"I'd rather hear that you'll start to stand up for yourself instead of feeling guilty because he's the way he is."

"I agree with Alex," Jules chimed in. "I didn't want to get physical, but he needed to be put in his place."

"Who was that anyway, an ex-boyfriend of yours?" I asked as I pretended like I didn't know her backstory.

"No offense, but you don't know me, so you don't need to know any of my personal business," Alora snapped. She didn't even look at me when she answered.

"Whoa! You can bite a complete stranger's head off for trying to make conversation, but you can't put Jordan in his place?" Jules argued.

"And *you* don't know me well enough to sit here and tell me how I should conduct myself."

"That's enough, Alora," Alex cut in. "Don't take your anger out on them. Fine, you don't know James, and he doesn't know you. But that doesn't give you the right to talk to him like that. And after what Jules just did, there's no way I'm going to sit here and let you talk to him like that either. Apologize."

Alora looked down at me and narrowed her eyes. I stared blankly back at her. This was my first time to get to see who she was as a person, face to face—not from a distance, on paper, or through a car window. So far, she wasn't making a good first impression. I was starting to regret wasting my time waiting on someone who seemed to be so toxic.

"Alora, apologize," Alex repeated.

She continued to stare at me as if she were trying to burn a hole through my face with her eyes. Then, she slowly looked to Jules. "I'm sorry I spoke to you in that tone, Jules. Listen, I'm heading home for the day. I'll see you tomorrow, Alex." She turned to walk away but stopped when Alex spoke.

"You forgot James," Alex pointed out.

"I don't know James, so I *didn't* forget anyone."

She quickly left the table before Alex could say anything else. After grabbing her things from the back room, she walked briskly to her car. She didn't look back as she got in, and she drove out of the parking lot. We all sat silently; we weren't sure what to make of what had just happened.

"James—"

"It's okay," I said, cutting Alex off. "I'll just assume this is what I get for handling things the way I did with her last night."

"That was out of character for her, though." Jules took Alex's soda and drank some of it.

Alex continued to try and get comfortable in the booth seat. "She's usually not like that. It's almost as though she was channeling Jordan. That was more like a stunt he'd pull."

"I'm sure she'll get home and realize what she did and feel bad about it," I shrugged.

The manager brought both lunch orders to the table, unaware that Alora had left for the day. After Alex explained to him what had happened and made a quick excuse as to why Alora had headed home, he allowed her to leave early so she could rest her leg and said she could make up for lost time throughout the week. I ended up eating what Alora had ordered so it wouldn't go to waste. Alex shared her lunch with Jules. Once we were finished, we walked on either side of Alex out of the diner. She struggled down the set of steps but made it without falling. Jules offered to give her a piggyback ride, but she turned it down. We took our time walking until we reached their cars.

"James, can you drive Alex's car and follow behind us so I can drive her home?" Jules opened the passenger door of his car for her, and she slid in slowly.

"Of course."

"I'm really sorry about all this, James." Alex adjusted the passenger seat from the reclined position it was in when I was sitting in it earlier and put her seat belt on as she stretched out her leg. "I really hope she realizes what she did and comes around."

"It's no big deal, really. It's only been a day since the breakup, so I wasn't expecting a welcoming party or anything. I'm sure it'll take time for her to warm up to me anyway." I leaned in, gave her a hug, and closed the door after she gave me her car keys from inside her purse.

After Jules dropped her off at home and they made up a bogus story as to why she was in more pain than usual to her parents, he and I headed out to the beach for a bit. I wished I'd brought my bodyboard and wetsuit jacket along with me. Going out into the water would have made me feel a hell of a lot better. Instead, I settled for sitting on the railing of the wooden deck to enjoy the breeze. Seagulls coasted by lazily as they scanned the beach for food. "I'm glad I'm not the one that froze up today," I chuckled as I sat on the wooden railing. I let my legs swing slowly after I got comfortable.

"That was worse than freezing up, to be honest. She's nothing like the person you saw at the diner today. I think she's just . . . I don't know. I don't want to make excuses for her, but I'm sure that if I thought hard enough, I'd be able to come up with one that fits the situation to a T." Jules plucked a small seashell over the edge of the railing he was sitting on and listened as it fell through the tall grass under us.

"I feel like I wasted my time waiting for her. She didn't seem too enthused to meet me," I confessed.

"Nah, you said it yourself. The breakup just happened yesterday, so it'll take time for her to get over it and warm up to you. The process *could* speed up if you sang to her through her bedroom window while playing a guitar, though."

Jules began to sing off-key at the top of his lungs. I winced and covered my ears. "You're destroying my eardrums over here," I said, smirking.

Jules laughed. "Seriously, though, I'm here to help, and you know Alex is, too—no matter how long it takes."

"My deadline is before the fall semester starts."

"Is that a personal deadline, or was that given to you?"

"Personal," I chirped.

"That's a pretty slim time frame, you know that, right?"

"I work better under pressure."

"Kind of like last night?"

I snickered and picked up a small pebble that was sitting near me on the railing and threw it at Jules. He caught it and dropped it in the grass where he had plucked the seashell.

"Hey, guys."

We both looked back toward the parking lot and fell silent. Jules cleared his throat and squared his shoulders, and then he turned back to face the beach. He gave me a side-glance and cleared his throat a second time. I took the hint, and I turned back to face the beach as well.

"Alora," Jules responded emotionlessly.

—Chapter 13—

About an hour after I left the diner, I received back-to-back calls from Alex. I watched as each one went to voice mail. For each call I didn't answer, she left a message. Then, a minute or two later, she called again. I knew she wouldn't stop until I answered and explained myself.

When she called me for what felt like the hundredth time, I took a deep breath and answered the phone. I didn't even get the chance to say anything before she started giving me the third degree. I listened to her in silence as I tossed Raven's favorite stuffed toy down the hallway for her to fetch and tossed it again every time she brought it back to me. Once Alex was finished scolding me, she started asking questions. After a few of them, she pretty much wore me down, and I started to answer them all the same way.

"How would you feel if someone treated you like that after we introduced you to them?"

"I don't know. It would depend on the person, I guess."

"That can't be your answer for everything, Alora. You *know* what you did was wrong, and—"

"I know, I know. I'm sorry, okay?"

"You're apologizing to the wrong person. You know *that*, too."

I threw Raven's toy farther down the hallway when she brought it back to me. It thumped against the linen closet door hard enough to startle her before she grabbed it. After eyeing it for a moment, she quickly snatched it away from the door and brought it back to me. "So what do you want me to do—track him down at some point and apologize?"

"You could have saved time and done that at the diner when I told you to. This is something you need to fix today. They went to the beach after they dropped me off at home since I was in no condition to drive. You'll find them there," Alex informed me.

My stomach sank. "*Them* meaning Jules is with him?"

"Yes. They're usually together when he's not with me. Jules doesn't know Matt and Sam well enough to hang around with them on his own yet, and even if he did, they're away on a camping trip for the summer anyway."

"C'mon, Alexia," I groaned as I slouched in the dining room chair and rested the back of my head on the top of the wooden backrest. "I've already changed into my bum-around clothes for the day, and I'm tired. I'm sure he'll be okay until I see him again."

"You don't know that. Besides, it doesn't matter what you're wearing. You're going there to apologize, not to appear on a catwalk in a fashion show."

"It wouldn't make a very good first impression to approach someone in an oversized T-shirt and sweatpants, I'm sure," I objected. I was trying my best to get out of having to leave my apartment.

"So you think the way you acted at the diner this afternoon was a good first impression?"

I snickered. "Touché." I got up from the table and walked to the front door to kick on a pair of old sneakers. When I dropped Raven's toy on the floor, she picked it up and tossed it around on her own. "Fine. I'll head out there after I change my shirt at least. It's too hot for the one I'm wearing anyway."

"It's too hot for the sweatpants, too. I just didn't say anything when you first told me that's what you're wearing," Alex chuckled.

I hung up with her after she told me what time we'd have to be at the diner the next day for more training. She wanted to make up for the time she had lost since she went home early that day because of the incident with Jordan, so I told her I'd be there with her, no matter how early or late she went to work the rest of the week. I figured I owed it to her. Plus, it'd help training go faster so I could start working on my own. After finding a clean tank top, I changed into it and tossed the T-shirt I had been wearing on the bed. I went out to the front room and turned the TV on for Raven.

"I'll be back in a bit, sweetheart. You be good."

I stooped over and patted her between the ears. She yawned and curled up in front of the TV with her stuffed toy so she could watch the dog show that started after the commercial break. After I grabbed my keys from the bowl by the front door and my purse off of the doorknob, I shoved my phone into my pocket and walked out into the breezeway. I quickly descended the stairs and trotted to my car after locking the door behind me. I wasn't sure how long Jules and his friend would be at the beach, but I didn't want to miss them. I knew I wouldn't hear the end of it from Alex if I got there and they were already gone.

I pulled into the parking lot at the beach and parked in my usual spot. I watched as a few people packed their cars to prepare to leave, while others were just arriving to spend the rest of the afternoon there. Jules's car was parked in front of the lone bathroom stall located by the steps that led up to the wooden deck that looked out to the beach. I could see two people sitting on the wooden railings and safely assumed they were them. After taking my phone out of my pocket and placing it in the center console, I took a deep breath, turned the car off, and slowly got out. I hooked one of the key loops onto my right index finger as I got closer to the steps. I could hear them talking to each other but couldn't make out what they were saying. I immediately began to panic when I realized I didn't remember Jules's friend's name. *It started with a J, I'm sure of it,* I thought. *There are too many J names floating around. It's getting confusing.*

They didn't hear me as I walked up the steps and made my way to them down the wooden walkway. I watched as Jules's friend picked up a small pebble and threw it at him. He caught it and dropped it over the side of the wooden railing. *The sooner you apologize, the sooner you can go back home.*

"Hey guys," I said.

They both looked back toward the parking lot and fell silent when they saw me. Jules cleared his throat and squared his shoulders, turning back to face the beach. He gave his friend a side-glance and cleared his throat a

119

second time. His friend took the hint, and turned back to face the beach as well.

"Alora," Jules responded emotionlessly.

I walked up and stood between them. They both continued to look out to the beach without saying a word. It was as if they were both wearing blinders.

"Let me know when you're ready to head back. I know you've got some sketches to work on," Jules said to his friend.

"Eh, I'm in no rush to finish. I'll have nothing to do afterward if I finish the last one tonight. I have a project I should really start for class, but that'll be a breeze," he responded.

They're acting as though I'm not here. I don't blame them. "Alex told me I'd find you guys here," I reported. "I just came by to apologize for my behavior at the diner. It was uncalled for."

Jules spun around to face me. He placed his feet on the wooden bench on the inside of the deck. "You already apologized to me. My issue is that you didn't apologize to James."

Thank God, *he said his name so I didn't have to fish for it.* "I'm sorry for the way I spoke to you at the diner,

James. I've been having a pretty rough couple of days, but that was no reason to snap at you the way I did."

James turned to face me as well. He eyed me in silence for a moment and then looked to Jules. "What do you think?" he inquired.

"I don't know . . . she *sounds* sincere. But I'm not sure we can trust someone who wears sweatpants in ninety-degree weather."

I blushed as I leaned forward and pushed his knee. "This is what I wear when I'm in the apartment most of the day. It's comfortable."

"Hey, whatever floats your boat," he laughed. "Her apology is legit, James. She wouldn't have said she was sorry if she didn't mean it."

James extended his hand to me. "Okay, let's try this again. I'm James Stone. And you are?"

"Alora Pebbles. Nice to meet you." I placed my hand in his and gave it a firm shake.

"See? This would have saved you time if you had done this at the diner earlier." Jules slid off of the railing and winked at me.

"That's the same thing Alex said when she insisted I come here to apologize." I let go of James's hand and began playing with a piece of thread that was coming loose at the bottom of my tank top. "You look awfully familiar. Have I seen you around before? What high school did you go to?"

"I went to the rival school not too far from yours. I don't believe we've met before." He looked as though he was trying to prevent himself from saying something I wasn't supposed to know; his eyes kept darting back from me to Jules and then back to me.

"You know," I said suspiciously, "I've never heard Alex or Jules talk about you. How long have you known them?"

"Oh, I don't know, a little over a year, I guess. That sounds about right, right, Jules?"

"It'll be two years for us starting fall semester. You'll still have a few months after that before it's two years for you and Alex," Jules corrected.

"So then, you met Alex when we weren't really on speaking terms?" I asked.

"I'm assuming so," James shrugged.

"That *seems* right. I noticed that Alex was hanging around with Jules a week after classes started our freshman year and was curious about what was going on. I never got to ask because Jordan insisted I mind my own business," I grumbled.

"I guess that answers the question I asked you at the diner," he said, smirking.

"Which was?"

"Whether or not the guy Jules had to set straight earlier today was an ex-boyfriend of yours." He slid off of the railing and stood off to the side.

"Oh . . . yeah, I'm *really* sorry about that." I took a step back and looked down at my sneakers. "Like I told Alex, if I had spoken up, none of that would have happened. I wanted him to go away—I *really* did—but I always freeze up when it comes to saying something to him."

"Well, I did the talking for you," Jules said. "We had just parked to come in to see you guys for your lunch break, so it's a good thing we got there when we did." Jules placed his hand on my shoulder and guided me to the steps that led down to the beach. "I think he's got some personal vendetta against me anyway, so something like that was probably bound to happen eventually."

The three of us found an area where the sand wasn't wet from the high tide. I sat between them—Jules to my left, and James to my right. For about an hour, we watched as a few kids ran up and down the beach and chased the seagulls while we made small talk. We laughed when a group of seagulls turned on the kids and chased them instead. They went screaming to their parents who were standing a few feet away, and they got scolded for harassing the birds.

"Thank you for accepting my apology," I said to James as I shoved my feet into the sand.

"It's water under the bridge," he assured me.

"I wish Alex could be out here with us. Instead, she's stuck at home until her leg stops hurting." Jules fell back into the sand so he could look up at the sky.

"Her physical therapy has been helping though, right? She told me that they said she should be as good as new by the time school starts back up again." I scooped up a handful of sand and let it run between my fingers.

"Well, yeah, that's true. But if she has more incidents like the one she had today, she'll have to keep going longer than they anticipated. She was only supposed to be in therapy for a year."

"We'll just have to make sure that what happened earlier doesn't happen again," James prompted.

"With any luck, what Jules did today will keep Jordan from coming around for a little while." I noticed it was getting late, so I decided it was time to head back home to get ready for work the next day. I slipped on my socks and sneakers and got to my feet. "I'm training again with

Alex at the diner tomorrow morning, so I should get going. You guys coming?"

"We're going to hang out here a little while longer." Jules continued to stare into the sky.

"I'll walk you to your car," James offered.

"Thanks."

We left Jules on the beach and made our way back to the parking lot in silence. It was nice to meet one of Alex's friends other than Jules, but I still didn't know him well enough to carry a conversation with him on my own. If he came around more with the group, it'd get easier. Until then, though, I figured it'd make things less awkward if I kept the conversation basic. Once we got to my car, he opened the door for me. It caught me by surprise, but I didn't say anything as I slid into the driver's seat. I checked my phone to see if I had any missed calls or texts, but there weren't any. I let out a sigh of relief as I set the phone back down on the page protector that the stranger at the beach the night before had slipped to me through the window.

"Thanks for walking me to my car." I closed the door and stuck the key into the ignition so I could roll the window down.

"Don't mention it."

"Do you go to the same college as us as well? I don't think I've ever seen you around campus before."

"I do, but I've been going part-time until recently. I'll be caught up to everyone after this summer class I'm taking. I actually plan on enrolling in my fall classes tomorrow before they all fill up."

"Okay, well, good luck with that. Maybe I'll see you around."

"Maybe," James said coolly.

I waved as I pulled out of the parking spot. I looked into my rearview mirror and noticed he was watching as I drove away. I couldn't help but feel as though the same thing had happened the night before. I assumed it was just a strong case of déjà vu and headed home.

—Chapter 14—

I quickly walked back to the beach once Alora's car was out of sight. There was so much running through my mind that I couldn't think straight. I had to get home to peruse the course catalog since I had no idea what classes I wanted or needed to enroll in. I wanted to do everything in my power to be around her as much as possible so nothing could go wrong, even if that meant enrolling in all of the classes *she* was enrolled in.

I spewed every idea I had once I sat back down next to Jules in the soft sand. He called Alex and had her on speaker phone so she could listen in on the conversation and give her opinion. Once I finished saying everything I had in mind for the next day, we started an open discussion on the one idea that seemed to make the most sense to me.

"You came up with this the second she left?" Alex asked. Jules turned the volume up on his phone so we'd be able to hear her over the crashing waves and squawking seagulls.

"Well, yeah," I admitted.

"You don't think she'll find it a bit odd that you're in every single class she's in?" Jules pointed out.

"You think she would?"

"Yes. I'm telling you right now, she'll think you're some creepy stalker person," Alex said matter-of-factly. "That's the first thing she'll say to me when she sees you walk into every classroom she's already sitting in. You two have completely different majors, so I think you need to consider taking only one or two of the same classes. Make sure you're taking a full course load for yourself, obviously, but be less obvious about what you're doing when it comes to her. You're overthinking it again."

"Plus, you gave yourself until *before* the semester starts to win her over. So doesn't waiting until then defeat the purpose of that deadline?" Jules added.

"I can change the deadline. It's not written in stone," I said defensively.

"Deadlines aside, you need to rethink this strategy of yours, James. Go home and write down the classes you want to take so that you can give the list to the counselor tomorrow. And *don't* rack your brain over which classes you think *she's* taking."

"Wait—do *you* two know what she registered for, or did you just hand her paperwork in this morning without looking at it at all?"

Jules's stare went blank, and he didn't answer my question. I heard Alex shift on the other end of the line, and she didn't answer my question, either.

"I should really get to bed since I have to go to work early tomorrow morning to train Alora. Talk to you guys tomorrow. Later."

Before I could object, Alex hung up the phone. Jules let out an exasperated sigh. He knew he couldn't avoid my question as easily as Alex had. "Well? Did you or did you not see which classes she enrolled in for the fall?"

He had no choice but to answer me. "James, I think Alex is right. Besides, her major has nothing to do with yours, so taking what she's taking would cause you to fall behind. You can't throw all this work away for a few hours of quality time with her every day."

"It's my choice. If that's what I want to do, then that's what I want to do. I can just take extra courses to keep up."

"So you're willing to take four classes or more every single day, all week—possibly on the weekend or online—not knowing if she'll even warm up to you?"

I knew Jules was right. "Well, then, what would you suggest?"

"The three of us are taking elementary Spanish together. We'll go to the counselor tomorrow to get your classes squared away and make sure you get put into the same class as us. That way, you can stay on track with your degree program and you two will have time to get to know each other better."

My stomach lurched at the thought of having to learn a foreign language. "Elementary Spanish? You guys couldn't go with something else?"

"Well, we *all* have to take a language course as a prerequisite. We figured Spanish would be easier, so that's what we went with. You'll be fine with all of us there, trust me."

The next afternoon, I met up with Jules in the campus courtyard. I had written down five classes to enroll in. The fifth was an alternate in case one of the other ones was full. I was reading over the crumpled piece of paper as we walked side-by-side toward the registration building.

"Excited to start taking classes that actually have to do with your major?" Jules laughed.

"Yeah, I'm really looking forward to this one computer course in particular. Imagine how much easier it'll be to make the license plates when all of this is said and done. I'll be a pro at it on a computer. I won't have to make designs by hand anymore."

"I actually like your sketches. But I agree; it'll be less messy after you learn the ins and outs of a few graphics programs." Jules opened the door and let me walk in first. We then followed the long hallway down to the office of the counselor we had been working with since our freshman year. Our pace slowed when we saw that the office door was cracked, and we heard frantic shuffling of papers and folders. "I wonder what she's doing." Jules pushed open the door slowly without knocking, and we both peered in. On the other side of the desk was a man who looked to be in his mid-thirties.

"Did you talk to this guy yesterday morning?" I whispered.

"No. I told you, our usual counselor was upset about having to handle Alora's registration since she's not her counselor and because she didn't get to talk to Alex about her classes, remember? I have *no* idea who this is."

We both walked in and approached the seats in front of the desk. The man behind it was too preoccupied with whatever he was looking for and didn't hear us enter. I looked to Jules. He looked to me and then shrugged. After a few more moments of watching the stranger in silence, Jules decided it was time to get his attention.

The man jumped when Jules cleared his throat loudly, and he spun around quickly to face us. "Oh, sorry. I didn't hear you two come in," he stammered. "What's your name?"

"Julian Reed. And you are?"

"Covering for your counselor." The stranger placed the stack of folders he was holding on the desk and quickly took a seat behind it.

"Okay . . ."

"Please, please, have a seat. Don't be shy."

Jules looked to me again. It didn't feel right speaking to a different counselor; he didn't know us—or *about* us. *This would be the perfect time for Alex to be here,* I thought. *Maybe she'd be able to read him and be able to tell if he's being honest or not.* I could tell Jules wasn't too comfortable with speaking to someone other than our usual contact, either. He shifted his weight as he tried to decide if he wanted to accept the invitation to have a seat or not.

"C'mon, fellas, I don't bite. You just caught me at a bad time, that's all," the stranger insisted.

"Then we'll come back another time." I patted Jules on the arm and headed toward the door to leave.

"Well, what I'm doing can wait," the man said. "Besides, your previous counselor fell ill. She won't be back for quite some time, so I'm your counselor for the time being. If this is in regard to your fall registration, you may want to take care of that now before all of the classes are full. You don't want to have slim pickings, right?"

I stopped dead in my tracks and looked at the list of classes in my hand. There was no guarantee that I'd get the one I really wanted now, which was the one with Jules, Alex, and Alora. But I wouldn't know if that would be possible or not unless I tried. "Right." I turned back, walked up to the desk, and handed the counselor the list.

"And your name, young man?" the counselor asked.

"James Stone."

"That's a strong name," he chuckled. He then quickly booted up his laptop and began typing away. It didn't take him long to print out a complete schedule for me. "Here you go, young man." The counselor handed it to me along with the list I had originally given him and then folded his hands on top of the desk. "Graphic design is a pretty interesting field. And just so you know, you're on track as far as your classes are concerned. Once you finish your art appreciation class in a few weeks, you'll be all caught up. Any particular reason as to why you were only going part-time for a while?"

"Personal reasons." I skimmed the schedule and saw that I was enrolled in an elementary Spanish course, but I wasn't sure if it was the one I was hoping to be placed in.

"Would you like to discuss those personal reasons with me? Maybe I can help."

"Um . . . no. I'm good, thank you."

"Okay, no problem. I'm not one to pry. I'll be here for the duration of the fall semester, so if you need anything, please feel free to stop by anytime. I'll be more than happy to assist you."

The counselor spun around in the chair and began digging through yet another drawer in one of the many filing cabinets against the back wall. Curious about what he was looking for, I crept closer to the desk to get a better look. Jules grabbed me by my arm, shook his head, and then gestured for us to leave. Without giving it a second thought, I followed him back out to the courtyard.

We didn't speak until we were outside the registration building.

"Did you sense anything about him?" Jules asked as he took the schedule out of my hand.

"He's not like us. That's the only thing I can tell you."

"Well, you had luck on your side today. You've got the same Spanish class with us. Congrats. I was holding my breath the entire time thinking this counselor change would ruin that for you."

"Right?" I took the schedule back and slipped it into my back pocket. "What do you have going on the rest of the day?"

"Well, Alex is still at work, which means I probably won't see her until later. I brought my schedule with me, so I'm heading to the campus bookstore now so I can get the textbooks I'll need. You?"

"I might as well go ahead and do the same thing since I'm here."

After getting the school materials we'd need and sitting down at our favorite burger shack for a while to eat, we headed back home. It was still early in the evening, but I had started a project the night before and needed to finish it soon. "You think we should tell

Alex about the counselor?" I asked as I took my newly purchased textbooks out of the trunk of my car.

"I don't know. Maybe we shouldn't say anything until she says something about having to go to the registration building. She'll just worry about it; she's got other things to focus on. He never did tell us his name, so I don't see the point. We wouldn't have much to tell her."

"You're right."

We said our good-byes on the second floor as Jules headed into his apartment. I went up to mine and placed the bag of textbooks by the front door. From there, I went over to the dining room table and started to wrap up my class project. The assignment was to draw an abstract piece to show a past or current situation we were in. I wanted to draw something that would describe my situation with Alora. I considered drawing some kind of scale that was broken but figured that'd be too complex. Then I thought about drawing a ship out at sea during a bad storm with a dim light from an SOS signal in the distance. I started that design but realized I'd end up using a lot of the primary colors I used for work, and I didn't want to go out and buy another box of pastels just yet. Just when I was ready to give up and go to bed, I thought of something. I took out all of the brightest pieces of pastel I had, grabbed the large canvas board I had purchased the day the final assignment was given to us, and got to work.

It only took me a few minutes to finish the project. I proudly held up the end product as I yawned loudly. "You've outdone yourself, James." I smeared a few of the colors a little more with my right thumb, scribbled my initials in the bottom right-hand corner, and then took it into my room for safekeeping. I wanted to make sure it wouldn't get messed up before it was due. Exhausted, I sluggishly crawled into bed and went to sleep.

—Chapter 15—

I paced back and forth in the back room where we
employees store our personal belongings during our
shifts. My thoughts were racing at a million miles a
minute. Rent was due at the end of the week, and I was
short. Then there was whether or not I should sign
another lease after my current one came to an end. I knew
the rental rate would be higher if I stayed another year,
so it was either struggle with that or go back to live at
home with my parents. I felt stuck and was on the verge
of having a panic attack. It had taken me only a week of
training with Alex to be on my own at the job. Since then,
time had flown by so fast. And even though I waitressed
like a rock star, I still wasn't able to make enough money
in the small window of time I had.

I jumped when Alex walked in and started to talk about her evening with Jules the night before. I took a seat and tried to listen to what she was saying, but all I heard was white noise. It was when she finished talking that she noticed I hadn't said anything to her since she arrived. "Alora? What's wrong?" She closed the locker she had put her purse in and put on her apron.

"Rent is due at the end of the week. I don't have enough to cover it."

She tied the apron strings behind her and took a seat next to me. "Well, I can spot you this time. You won't have to pay me back or anything."

"I also don't know if I should sign a lease for another year," I groaned. "You may not know this, but rental rates go up a small percentage every time you renew. And who knows what other fees will get tagged on to it."

"Oh . . . well, that's something I *can't* help you with," she sighed. "How about after work, we go meet up with the guys so we can try and figure something out?"

Ever since they had introduced me to James, he had been around more—a *lot* more. Carrying on a conversation with him was still touch and go, but I was getting used to his being around. It took the pressure off of me when it came to being the third wheel when I went out with Alex and Jules. "Sure. Maybe they'll have some good ideas."

I rode with Alex to the school campus the next day. She arranged for all of us to meet in the courtyard since it was our day off. We hadn't had time to meet up with James and Jules the night before because we had ended up working a double shift. We hoped that would help make a little more money, which it did, but not enough to cover what I didn't have. The three of us sat patiently on one of the concrete tables as we waited for James to show up.

"What's taking him so long?" I started anxiously picking at my fingers.

"Relax, Alora. The rent is due tomorrow, not today. We'll figure something out. When is the deadline to renew the lease?" Alex asked as she stopped me from destroying my cuticles and nails.

"Tomorrow."

"This is quite a tight spot you've gotten yourself into," Jules pointed out. "It's okay though. Like Alex said, we'll figure something out."

We all fell silent when we saw James approaching us from across the courtyard. He was carrying a large piece of canvas at arm's length as if he didn't want to touch whatever was on it. When he got to us, he gently placed it face up on top of the table after we moved so there was room for it.

"How'd it go?" Jules asked as he looked on.

"What kind of a question is that?" James smirked, pulled a folded piece of paper from his pocket, and handed it to Jules.

I looked down at what he had placed on the table and cocked my head to the side. "Is this supposed to be a drawing of—pick-up sticks?" I wanted to touch it, but whatever the drawing was done with looked very fresh, so I didn't want to smear it. His initials were scribbled in the lower right-hand corner.

"That's exactly what it's a drawing of," he confirmed.

"What was the assignment? Awesome grade, by the way." Jules handed the piece of paper back to him.

"Thanks. We were instructed to draw something abstract about a current situation in our lives."

"Why pick-up sticks, though?" Alex asked.

"Well, maybe he's going through something that's a bit of a mess right now, or maybe he knows someone who's having problems," I began. "To him, the mess or problem is like this pile of colorful sticks he drew. Since, you know, that's what these damn things look like when you drop them on the floor or on a table to play the game—know what I mean? Anyway . . . he's probably working to pick up as many as he can before the mess or problem gets worse or before someone beats him to the punch. Am I right? Or at least close?"

"That was, actually, pretty spot-on." James sounded impressed. "I described it a little differently when I presented it today, but what you said works, too."

"C'mon, let's get it in your car so it doesn't get messed up. I'm sure you'd like to frame it since it helped you get the grade that got you caught up with your credits." Jules lifted one side of it; Alex beat James when it came to grabbing the other side.

"I'll help him," she offered.

"You don't think you're too short?" James chuckled.

"Shut up," she shot back with a laugh.

Alex and Jules talked quietly to each other while James and I followed behind them. James looked straight ahead; it looked as though he was deep in thought, so I wasn't sure if saying something to him would break that train of thought or not. He quickly snapped out of it when he noticed that I glanced at him. "So you really like the picture?" he asked shyly.

"I think it's amazing. I can't believe you did that yourself. You're really talented."

"Thanks. I come up with designs for custom plates at the booth I work at in the flea market. I've had a lot of time to perfect my craft."

"I wasn't aware that you worked with Jules. I guess there's a lot I need to learn about you, huh?"

"There isn't much, really." He pulled out his car fob and unlocked the doors as we got closer to it.

"Where do you want it, sir?" Alex asked as they slowed to a stop.

"The back seat is fine. It shouldn't make a mess or anything back there," James instructed.

Jules opened the back door and handled the canvas from there. Alex took a step back to give him room. Moments later, he was done placing it safely on the back seat. "I'm glad you're on track now. You won't have to stress over getting caught up before the fall. Now you have the rest of the summer to have fun with us."

"Yeah, it's definitely a huge relief." James leaned on the side of his car.

"Okay, guys, there's an important matter at hand here." Alex turned to look at all of us. "Alora is short with her rent and isn't sure whether or not she should renew the lease. I've offered to pick up the slack this time, but this could possibly become an ongoing problem for her.

And apparently, the rent goes up a small percentage when you renew."

James nodded. "That's true."

"Whose name is on the lease anyway?" Jules asked.

The three of them looked at me, and they all sighed at the same time when they saw the look I gave. My facial expression answered the question without my having to say anything.

"That's going to be a problem. Depending on how strict the complex is, they may not let you renew the lease since it's in Jordan's name." Jules dropped his head back and shut his eyes.

"So the rent will be taken care of, but she could *still* end up out on the street or back at home with her parents?" Alex sat on the hood of James's car and looked at the concrete as she fell into deep thought. Soon after, James spaced out. I could tell they were all trying to figure something out once they realized that my problem was bigger than we had initially thought it was. I watched the three of them as they thought quietly to themselves. I was grateful for their help, but if they weren't able to come up with any suggestions, it would mean that I would either have to get Jordan to renew the lease for me and struggle with rent I could barely afford or go back to living with my parents.

Without warning, James stood straight up excitedly, which caused his car to shake gently. "Why don't you and Alex get a place together?"

"Why didn't I think of that?" Alex said happily. "Alora, this is great! I think that's the best solution to your problem. Think about it."

I pictured how it'd be to see her every day outside of work and school, and how much easier it would be to pay rent since we'd be splitting it down the middle. "That's actually an amazing idea."

"We can help you move," Jules added. "Maybe by then, Matt and Sam will be back from their camping trip and they can help, too."

"Help with what?"

The four of us turned to see Jordan approaching us. None of us were sure if he was walking by and just happened to hear us talking or if he had made a beeline when he saw us together to find out what we were doing.

"I'm short with rent for tomorrow, and the lease is up, too. We were talking about what I could do to fix the problem," I told him.

"Why are you explaining yourself to him?" Alex slid off of the hood of James's car and stood next to me.

"Well, what if he was able to talk the leasing office into freezing the rate and renewed the lease for me so I could stay another year?"

"But you *just* said moving in with Alex was an amazing idea," Jules argued from behind us.

"Listen, I like to think of myself as a pretty persuasive person and all," Jordan said, "but I can't just walk into the front office and insist they not jack up a rate for anyone, not even for me. So even if I *did* want to renew the lease for you, you'd just have to deal with what they charge you monthly."

"So you knew this would happen? That if your name was on the lease and not hers, she'd have to leave regardless of whether you two were still together if you didn't want to renew?" Alex asked.

"Of course I did," Jordan grinned. "I figured it'd teach her the importance of doing things on her own and not accept everything that was handed to her."

"You're a real piece of work," I managed to get out.

Jordan put his hand close to my face and began rubbing his middle finger against his thumb. "You see this? This is me playing the world's saddest song on the world's smallest violin."

Alex slapped his hand out of my face. "Get out of here."

Jordan chuckled and sashayed away without saying another word. When I was sure he was out of earshot, I emitted a quiet shout as I balled my hands into fists. "I wasted *so* much time on him! When did he turn into such a tool?"

"Who knows, and who cares." James pushed between me and Alex so he could look at me face to face. "You don't need him. You have *us*, right?"

"R—right," I stammered.

"Okay. So this is what's going to happen," James continued. "Alex will help you with your rent, so you won't have anything to worry about when it comes to that, okay?"

I stared at him and was at a loss for words. "Okay."

"Alex?" James turned to her.

"I'm listening," she said.

"Alora probably has a week to stay there after she tells the front office that she won't be renewing the lease. Maybe you can help her talk them into letting her stay there an extra week or two until we can get things squared away with a new place. Then you should probably go over the specifics with your parents to let them know what's happening. I'll take Jules with me to apartment hunt for you guys. We'll have something for you two to look at by tomorrow afternoon at the latest, okay?"

"Got it," Alex chirped happily.

"I'll try and get a hold of Matt to let them know what they'll be coming back to. That way we'll know if we'll have two extra sets of hands to help with the move." Jules pulled out his cell phone and stepped off to the side to make the call.

"Come on, Alora," Alex said. "We have to get to the bank so I can get the rest of the money you need to pay your rent. We might as well get that out of the way today so we'll have one less thing on our minds tomorrow at work. We can talk to our parents today too if you'd like." Alex turned away and made her way to her car. I continued to stare at James.

"Thank you." I gave him a huge hug, which was something he wasn't expecting. "I owe you one. I really do."

He hugged me back after a moment of being surprised. "I'll hold you to that. We'd better get going. I've got a couple of complexes in mind that you and Alex may like. Don't hesitate to give me a call if you run into any issues."

"Okay."

I walked over to Alex's car and got in. After putting on my seat belt, she began driving. "This is exciting," I said.

"Yeah, it is," Alex agreed as she headed toward the bank. "It was nice of James to offer to look for a place with Jules for us. I'm sure they'll find something affordable."

"That *was* nice of him," I said with a hint of suspicion. "What's his angle?"

"*Angle?*" Alex laughed loudly. "There's no angle. James is just a really nice guy who likes to do really nice things for really nice girls."

"Has he done really nice things for *you?*"

"I already have someone to do nice things for me," she laughed. "Don't put too much thought into it or anything, but if I were you, I'd look at this as the silver lining finally appearing in the clouds."

I smiled to myself. I couldn't help but wonder if my beach ritual was actually contributing to the events unfolding. If it was, I was glad that I hadn't abandoned the idea that I thought was ridiculous for so many years.

—Chapter 16—

I watched as Alora walked over to Alex's car and got in. When they were out of sight, I walked up to Jules as he wrapped up his call with Matt.

"He said they'd be happy to help. They'll be back just in time for the move," Jules confirmed.

"Good. I didn't think the two of us alone would be able to get all of their things into an apartment in one day."

"You definitely gained some cool points for coming up with the idea of them living together." He put his phone back into his pocket.

"I'm surprised you and Alex didn't come up with that first." I looked at him before getting into my car and saw a mischievous smile on his face. "Wait—"

"We came up with it a while ago when we found out that Jordan took her money stash while the three of us were out to lunch. We just figured we'd wait and see how the whole thing played out and let you make the suggestion. In all honesty, Alora should have been the one to come up with the idea and run it by Alex, but I think she has a problem with asking for help." Jules got into his car and rolled down his window. "You're taking charge, though, with helping her—that's all that matters. I saw the look on her face. She was impressed. So don't lose steam now. We've got apartment hunting to do."

"Hunting? We're only going to one place." I got in my car and rolled down the passenger window so we could bring our conversation to a close until we reached our first and only apartment destination.

Jules thought about it for a second and smirked. "I've said it once, and I'll say it again: you're crafty."

"Saying that I'm crafty gives me *too* much credit. Like I said, I just know how to use my resources."

After sitting and talking with the leasing office manager at our complex, we had a move-in date for a two-bedroom, two-bathroom apartment on the other side of the property. We got to do a walk-through and chose the floor level for them as well.

"It'll be a pain lugging all their stuff up here for them, but I think the third floor is the best choice," I insisted.

"I get why you think that, but we should also keep Alex's leg in mind. I think we should keep them on the second floor," Jules countered.

"Can't putting them on the third floor be considered extra exercise that she'd do at a therapy session anyway?"

"Are you trying to be funny, or are you being serious?" he asked sternly.

"You know I wouldn't joke about that. You *also* know that if we put them on the first floor, she'll think that we don't think she can handle the stairs. And she'll find some reason to look at you crooked if you suggest the second floor. Besides, if it's a problem, we can change it before we move them in, right?" I looked to the manager and he nodded in agreement. "See?"

"I guess . . . Okay, the third floor it is."

The next day, we went to see Alex and Alora at the diner to show them what we had found and to grab some breakfast before we headed to work. I had the paperwork nicely tucked in a folder for them to look through while we were eating. They only had a few minutes to sit with us and go over everything, so once our food was brought to us, I handed the folder across the table to them.

"I think you guys will be happy with the monthly rate and the location." I watched as Alora leafed through the papers before handing them to Alex. "If you guys take a look at the unit and you don't like it for whatever reason, they can change it for you."

"Can I take this with me to show my parents after work?" Alora asked.

"Sure, if it'll give them peace of mind."

"Great. I'll be right back."

She got up and headed in the direction of the restroom. Alex began sluggishly leafing through the folder. She didn't seem as enthused as she had the day before.

"Everything okay, Alex?"

She looked up at me from the papers and stifled a yawn. She looked like she had been up all night. "I'm fine. I'm just exhausted. I haven't been getting much sleep lately."

"She's been getting really bad headaches the past few days. She's also been having nightmares that seem to be getting worse." Jules leaned in closer to the table and dropped his voice to a whisper. "At first I thought it may have something to do with her gift—whatever it is. But now, I'm not so sure."

"Do you remember what the nightmares are about or when they started?" I asked.

"I remember bits and pieces but not enough to tell you what they're about exactly. They probably started about a week ago. I usually have nightmares here and there; they've just become more frequent lately. Let's not make a big deal out of it, okay? I'm trying not to."

"If you insist. I suggested that the apartment you guys are moving into be on the third floor. Is that okay? If it's asking too much of your leg and all, like I said, the complex will change it for you."

"The third floor is fine." Alex closed the folder and sat it on the table in front of Alora's seat. "It'll be extra exercise since I'll be finished with therapy soon."

I lightly kicked Jules under the table, and he shook his head. "Yeah, yeah, yeah. You were right; I was wrong," he admitted.

Alora came back to the table and picked up the folder so she could leaf through it again. "Will Matt and Sam be able to help with the move?"

"I talked to Matt yesterday, and he said they'd be more than happy to help," Jules reported.

"What about a deposit and things of the like? Are there any application fees?"

"That's all been taken care of," I assured her.

"By you, or—?"

"Oh, no," I laughed. "They were running a special for new applicants. You two will still have to go in and fill out the paperwork and all, but the rest of the stuff is covered after they approve everything."

"So three weeks from today we'll be sharing an apartment. I know I don't sound excited, but I really am." Alex reached over and took a piece of Jules's toast. She took a bite of it and chewed it sleepily.

"Thank you so much again, James." Alora smiled at the folder. I could tell she was letting her thoughts roam about this new adventure she was about to embark on.

"Anything to help."

After breakfast, I rode with Jules to work. When we got there, our boss sat us down to talk to us about the suggestion we had made regarding changing the prices of the license plates and frames. "I think it's a good idea, but I want to do it when you're finished with school, James.

Once you have some extra training and knowledge under your belt, maybe I'll turn the booth over to you and you can run it yourself. You've been kind of like an apprentice since you started here, so I'd be honored to give you full control when the time is right."

I was shocked and pleasantly surprised. "Thank you, sir. You don't know how excited I am about all of this. I'll make you proud, I promise."

That evening, I lay in my bed and stared at the ceiling. Everything that had transpired since the day before had me on a natural high. Just as I was about to slip into a deep sleep, an idea for an apartment-warming gift for Alora crossed my mind. I made a mental note to price frames at the flea market the next day while on lunch break. "You've outdone yourself yet again, James," I yawned to myself.

—Chapter 17—

"I don't want to throw it away because it's a really nice box, but I don't think it can be fixed." I held up the lid and the base of the keepsake box that had broken when I threw it against the wall in my previous apartment for Sam to see. "What do you think?"

Sam placed one of my many full cardboard boxes in the far corner of my room in the new apartment and took both pieces out of my hand. After looking at it for a couple of seconds, she tossed both pieces on the bed. "I think you should worry about that box after you're settled in." She grabbed my arm and dragged me out of the room.

The guys were working on bringing the dining room table through the front door. Jules and Matt struggled as James gave them directions. "If you'd just turn it a little to the side, it'd come in just fine."

"This is harder than it looks, James," Jules said through gritted teeth. "This table isn't light, and I'm ready to assume it'll never get through this stupid door." He set his end down on the ground and leaned on one of the legs.

Matt sat his end down too. "He's right. I've got half a mind to go grab a saw and cut this thing in half."

"But it got into her old apartment just fine. If it fit through that door, it should fit through this one, too," James reasoned.

I walked up to the table and looked at where the legs were attached. "Here's your problem." I grabbed the fattest part of one of the legs and began to twist it until it came off. I held it up for the three of them to see. "The legs are removable."

The three of them looked at me and began shaking their heads.

"What? I wasn't home when this stuff was delivered and assembled." I squeezed between the table and the door frame to get outside; Sam followed and we headed down to the moving truck. We giggled when we heard Jules and Matt mumble to themselves as they began to unscrew the other three legs off of the table. "I honestly didn't know," I whispered to Sam.

"I believe you," she laughed. "You know, James seems like a really nice guy."

"So far, yes." I hopped off the last step onto the sidewalk. "You don't think he's a little *too* nice?"

"I understand your apprehension, but this is a good change for you. Things seem to be falling into place slowly but surely. I'm happy for you."

"Aw, thanks, Sam."

We walked up to the moving truck where Alex was sitting. She wanted to help, but Jules had insisted that she stay put and make sure no one took anything from the truck when we weren't there. "Did they get the table inside?" she asked.

"After they unscrew all of the legs from the base, it'll go in just fine." Sam hopped inside of the truck and sat next to Alex. She let her legs swing lazily off the edge after she got comfortable. "We're making good time, though. Will you need help unpacking anything once everything is inside?"

"No. But I'd like to be able to do *something* to help when it comes to this move. Everyone is treating me like I'm fine china."

I looked inside of the truck at Raven. She was sitting quietly in a far corner, hidden in the shadows. It was hot out, so she had found a way to stay cool and out of everyone's way at the same time. "You can walk Raven up so she can take a look around. I'm sure that's something you won't get the third degree for since you're technically not moving anything." I whistled to Raven, and she walked up and stood between Sam and Alex. She looked like she was ready to take a nap. "Let me go grab her leash out of my car. I'll be right back."

I shielded my eyes from the glaring sun as I dug into my pocket to get the keys, slowing my pace when I saw someone standing by my car. My stomach sank when I recognized who it was.

"How's the move going?" Jordan asked smugly as I pushed by him to get to the passenger side of the car where Raven's leash was.

"Why are you here, Jordan?" I sighed.

"I'm here to get my stuff."

I didn't bother unlocking the car when he answered. "What stuff?"

"The furniture you're moving into your place—*that* stuff. It's mine."

"Now wait a minute. You *gave* all of that to me for the apartment I was staying in!"

"Yeah, an apartment that was in *my* name that *I* paid for every month," he jeered. "I never said, 'Here you go, Alora. Have some free furniture.' I only got it so you'd have a furnished place and a bed to sleep on. I'm not *that* heartless."

"But you're heartless enough to come here and take it back? We've moved just about everything in already. You can't do this! You don't even have room for any of it!"

"All it'll take is one call to a professional moving company, and they'll come get everything so your friends don't scuff any of it. I can just sell it to make my money back. Or maybe I'll replace some of my old furniture with it."

I watched as he pulled out his phone and prepared to call whoever it was he had in mind to come and get all of the furniture we had worked hours to get up three flights of stairs. I tried to think of something to say to make him reconsider, but the only thing I could think to do was text James so he'd come down and try to help me reason with him. I pulled out my phone as well and did just that, and then I put it back in my pocket after I sent the message.

"Who'd you text, Mommy and Daddy?" Jordan said, mocking me.

"What's going on?"

It was James. He made it down just before Jordan pushed the call button. He had trotted over to us and stood by me as he caught his breath. *That was fast*, I thought.

"I'm here to get my furniture," Jordan said curtly.

James wiped the sweat from his forehead. "Well *that's* not happening. We worked all day getting that stuff up there. If you wanted it so badly, you should've said something when you found out she planned on moving in the first place. You're out of luck."

"No, Alora's out of luck. I paid for that furniture, so it's mine."

"You don't even know if you'll keep any of it. You said you might sell it all," I argued.

"Really?" James went into his back pocket and fished out his wallet. "How much did you plan on selling it for?"

Jordan's face went stone cold. "You can't afford it."

"Try me," James challenged.

They stared each other down; neither of them moved a muscle. I could tell the gears in Jordan's head were working at full speed. I knew he wouldn't come up with a ridiculous amount, but I also knew that he'd come up with an amount that was higher than what he had originally paid. No one would be able to challenge him on it because we had no idea what he had paid when he first bought everything.

"Thirty-five hundred," Jordan finally barked.

"For a queen-sized bedroom set, dining room table, and front room furniture?" James said with a raised brow.

"It's high-quality furniture."

"I'm not saying it isn't." James dug into his wallet and pulled out a blank check. "Alora, do you have a pen in your car?"

I didn't hesitate to unlock the car and grab one from the glove compartment along with the leash I had originally gone to the car to retrieve. They were still staring each other down as I handed him the pen. He leaned against the passenger window and quickly filled out the check, signed the bottom, and handed it to Jordan.

"I threw in a few extra bucks to cover the gas you wasted coming over here for nothing."

Jordan quickly folded the check and shoved it into his back pocket. "It had better not bounce."

"Trust me, it won't."

"Remember what I told you about taking handouts, Alora. Someone won't always be around to get you out of a situation just because you don't know how to handle it yourself." Jordan quickly walked to his car and left. I locked my car door and got the leash ready for Raven.

"You ever consider getting a restraining order on him?" James asked as we walked back to the moving truck.

"No, I don't think it'll be necessary to take it *that* far. He's just being Jordan; there's no changing that."

"Well, we finally got the dining room table inside. All that's left now are a few more boxes, and you guys will be set."

"Thanks . . . so can we *not* say anything to Alex or Jules about what just happened?"

"On one condition." He pulled my arm to stop me from walking just as we were about to go around to the back of the moving truck. I could hear Matt and Jules talking to Sam and Alex as they played with Raven.

"Which is?"

"Alex will probably talk to you about it tonight, but she told me she's working on putting something together for us to do as a group before the fall semester starts. I'd like to escort you to—whatever it is she comes up with."

"What if it's something small, like just the six of us getting together for dinner?"

"I'd like to escort you."

"Okay . . . what about if she were getting all of us together to go to her *parents* for dinner?"

"I'd like to escort you," he said in the same tone.

"What if . . . she led all of us off of a short cliff?"

"You'd be on your own with that—unless you asked me to set up a nice, soft landing pad at the bottom for you, then I'd be more than happy to do that," he chuckled.

"And that's all you want? Is there a catch or something? You don't want me to pay you back for all of the furniture you just paid for or anything?"

"I know it sounds a bit suspicious, but no. You don't have to pay me back, and I promise you I won't try to claim any of it if you decide to move out next year. All I want is your time."

He placed his hand out so we'd shake on it, which seemed a little impersonal. We had hung out a few times, just the two of us, as the move got closer, which I figured would ease any tension or awkwardness between us. But he was still nervous around me, even when we were out with Alex and Jules. So I figured that we'd just need a little more time around each other before he was 100 percent comfortable. "Okay," I said, "it's a date."

Alex invited everyone over to our place for dinner that night so we could cook for them to show our appreciation for helping us move and to break in the kitchen for the first time. After everyone went home to freshen up, they came back to find pasta and breadsticks waiting for them. When everyone was served and seated, the conversation began to flow. It felt good to have amazing people around to enjoy the moment with. Raven was sound asleep under her favorite chair in the front room.

"Any crazy stories you guys want to share from your camping trip?" Alex asked Matt and Sam.

"Nothing out of the ordinary. We had fun as usual. We learned how to scale a few rock walls and how to track things. That was different from last year, but that's about it," Matt said as he twisted his fork in his pasta.

"You know, I don't know when we'll ever need to use any of those skills," Sam pointed out. "It's not like we have that kind of forestry around here. We'd probably only have to walk a mile or two in the woods if we got lost and we'd be back in civilization, or close enough to it."

"I don't think there's anything wrong with having some level of survival skills under your belt, though." Jules placed his cup on the table after taking a drink from it.

"Speaking of survival skills," Sam said excitedly, "while we were at the registration building the other day to enroll for our fall classes, we found a flyer advertising a group survival workshop or challenge of some kind. I signed us all up for it. The list is pretty long, though. A lot of people signed up."

"I don't want to go out on a survival *anything*," Alex objected. "You should have asked us first before volunteering anyone. You and Matt are the only ones who know anything about being out in the wilderness."

"Relax, you big baby. Like I said, a lot of people signed up, so our group may not make the cut. The date of the drawing is still to be determined anyway, so it may not happen for a while—or at all."

"I don't know. I think I'd like to go on something like that. It'd be an amazing experience for all of us." James wiped his mouth and placed the napkin on his empty plate.

"I agree. I'd actually think of it as a vacation depending on where we end up," I chimed in.

When we all finished eating, we sat in the front room for a few hours and watched a couple of movies that Jules had brought over. We were all paired off, which felt weird at first. But it was nice to be able to hang out with someone like James. I didn't have to worry about him complaining about how bored he was seeing as how he got along with everyone, and vice versa.

"Did you figure out what you wanted to do with that broken box of yours?" Sam asked after the last movie was over. Everyone was preparing to leave for the night.

"I actually forgot about it. I may just throw it away. I really don't think it can be fixed."

"James may be able to fix it," Jules blurted out.

I looked at James, and he was giving Jules the evil eye.

"What? Don't be so modest." Jules stood and stretched.

"Do you think you can, James?" I asked.

"What kind of box is it?"

I got up from the couch and grabbed the lid and base off of my bed. He took them from me when I brought them out to him.

"Did this happen during the move today?"

"No, I kind of got angry and threw it against the wall at the old apartment when I found out that the money that was inside of it had been taken."

He smirked as he took a closer look at the hinge. "I'll see what I can do."

After wishing everyone a good night, I helped Alex clean up the kitchen. It was nice having someone other than Raven around for once. I was beginning to think I was going to go crazy because of the lack of social interaction.

"I know that box was a gift from Jordan when you guys were actually getting along, but I think you should just get rid of it." Alex placed the dirty dishes in the dishwasher after rinsing them off and started it. "We can always find something else for you to put keepsakes in, you know."

"It's such a unique piece, though."

"There's nothing unique about a wooden box with your initials engraved in the lid, Alora. You can get something like that made anywhere for the right amount of money. That's probably what Jordan did."

"Okay, well, if James can't fix it, then I'll throw it away. Deal?"

"Deal. Also, I was thinking the six of us could get together and go to the fair that'll be in town before school is back in session. What do you think?"

Every year, a fair came to town and left before school started. We had been going for years, with the exception of the last two because of everything that had been going on. We also had never gone as a group of couples before because of the situation I was in with Jordan and the fact that Alex hadn't been with anyone whenever we tried to get that idea to take off when someone suggested it.

"It sounds like a good idea. It'd be a new experience for Jules since he's not originally from around here, and it's inexpensive. Maybe I can pay for James's admission ticket or something."

"So you plan on asking him to go *with* you for this occasion?" Alex made kissy faces at the ceiling and batted her eyes.

I threw a dishtowel at her face. "Maybe," I answered shyly. "Maybe we already know we're going together regardless of what you came up with for the group."

"Well, I think that's great. You two will definitely have a great time with each other. I know it."

I checked my phone when it vibrated from a text message. I smiled to myself when I read it. "James wants to know if I'd like to go with him to the beach Monday afternoon."

"You're off work that day, so if I were you, I'd go."

I didn't hesitate to accept his invitation.

—Chapter 18—

"The *last* thing I want to do is fix something that *he* gave her." I gave Jules a playful shove as we looked at a few keepsake boxes in one of the booths at the flea market while we were on our lunch break. "Thanks for volunteering me, though," I said sarcastically.

"If I didn't, you would have missed out on the perfect opportunity to score some additional cool points." Jules picked up a cherry wood box, opened it, and then placed it back on the shelf. "What're we looking for exactly? You've already found a frame for her apartment-warming gift."

"I'm trying to find a box that's the same wood grain as the one I'm supposed to fix. I can connect the lid to the base after getting the necessary pieces, but the impact damaged the lid pretty badly. That's something I *can't* fix without messing up the engraving. I figure it'd be easier for me to just get a replacement box for her and get her initials engraved in it so it's like the original since she likes it so much." I pushed a couple of boxes to the side to see if there were any better-looking ones in the back.

"May I make a suggestion?"

"You may."

"I think you should put your craft to work with this project."

I raised a brow as I put the boxes I had moved to the side back in their original places. "Go on," I said curiously.

"Why not make a new and improved *custom* lid? If the base is fine, take one of these blank keepsake boxes, swap the lid out, and design something on it yourself. It'd make it a *truly* unique piece, you know? I'm sure Jordan just took the original somewhere and paid to get her initials engraved into it, which is fine if you're a minimalist. But if you give it your personal touch, it'll be *better* than the original because you went the extra mile. She'll look at it and say, 'James *made* this for me,' which is better than,

'Jordan *got* this for me.' That's just my personal opinion. You can do what you want," Jules shrugged.

"That's actually a *really* good idea," I said as I grabbed what looked to be a box with wood grain close enough to the original box. We walked up to the front counter and waited in a short line so I could pay for it, along with a large wooden frame I had found when we first got there. "You think this one is close enough to the original?"

Jules took the box out of my hand, looked at it, and then handed it back to me. "I think it's close enough for her to not notice anything different other than what you engrave yourself."

"I know exactly what design I want to use, too. You won't tell her what I'm doing, right?"

"Nope. This is all on you now, so whatever you decide to do from here on out is entirely up to you. I'll support whatever you decide to do as long as it isn't crazy."

"Are Alex's nightmares getting worse?" I handed the cashier cash to pay for the items. She carefully wrapped the box in tissue paper and then placed it in a plastic bag. She then moved on to wrap the picture frame in pieces of brown paper.

"Every time I ask her about them, she gets snippy and changes the subject. You think something's going on that she's not telling us?"

"The whole near-death thing can be pretty traumatic; it's different for every person who experiences it. It may take her years to work through whatever is going on and to get used to whatever gift she came back with."

"How'd *you* learn to cope?"

"I talked about it with my parents to a certain extent. I talk to you about it in depth whenever I feel the need to."

"What about when I wasn't here?"

"It was difficult. There were times when I was ready to rip myself apart when I couldn't understand what I was feeling or what was going on, know what I mean? But I took my time to take control of what it was and worked it out on my own. In the end, I figured out that I had a gift and what my gift was, and I've learned to live with it ever since. When she's ready to talk, I'm sure she will; then we can help her. Just give her time."

I took the bag that contained my newly purchased item after I was given my receipt, and Jules carried the frame for me as we made our way out of the booth. We stopped at a food stand and purchased a couple of corn dogs and some drinks. After grabbing a few packets of mustard and straws, we spent the rest of our lunch enjoying our food. The smell of freshly spun cotton candy and powdered funnel cake hung in the air.

"You know what I haven't heard you talk about in a while?" Jules wiped his mouth and dropped the now empty corn dog stick onto the plastic tray it had come on.

"Nope," I said with my mouth full.

"You haven't said anything about finding buried items at the beach from Alora."

I thought about it as I finished my corn dog. I took a sip of soda as I tried to remember the last time I had noticed any colorful shells out there that marked where she had buried something. "You're right."

"Have you just stopped checking?"

"I've been out there a few times since you introduced me to her, but going about my usual routine when I'm there honestly hasn't crossed my mind in a while. Do you think she's stopped going out there to do that?"

"Maybe," Jules said as he grabbed a clean napkin and wiped his mouth again.

I wasn't sure if that was a good thing or a bad thing. I was so wrapped up in trying to get to know her that I hadn't noticed a change in her behavior—or my own—when it came to that. "What if there are dozens of buried letters and poems and lists out there and I've been overlooking them?" I gasped.

"I think you're fine," Jules assured me. "She hasn't said anything to me or Alex about going out there, so maybe she just hasn't felt the need to."

"I guess I'll find out tomorrow. I'll try not to think about it until then."

"What's going on tomorrow?"

After we cleaned up around ourselves, we slowly made our way back to *Plates & Frames R Us.*

"When I got home last night from dinner at their place, I asked Alora if she wanted to come out to the beach with me tomorrow. She accepted the invite."

"Oh, nice," Jules said as we split apart to let an older couple walk between us. We entered *Plates & Frames R Us* and weaved between the wooden tables where dozens of booklets that contained different frame and plate designs to choose from lay. After Jules put the frame in the back where I worked, he got situated behind the front counter. "I'm sure once you two get out there, you'll realize that there was nothing to panic about. If she hasn't buried anything, that means what you're doing is working. Then you can give yourself a pat on the back. Until then, try not to stress over it; we've only got a few hours left to fill these orders, so you've got to focus."

I grabbed my black apron from under the counter and tied it around my waist. "You're right. Thanks for helping me stay grounded through all of this."

"Just doing my job," Jules said, smiling.

—Chapter 19—

"I don't know about this . . ."

I anxiously gripped the bodyboard I was lying on as we floated in the open water. I could still see the shore, but not being able to feel the sand beneath my feet had me on edge.

James looked behind us as a small wake-sized wave came in and caused us to tip to the side. "You'll be fine," he said as he wiped some water from his face. "Just do what I told you, and you'll coast right back to shore."

"But what if I fall off?" I grabbed his hand just as he was about to push away from me.

"You'll be okay," he laughed. "The waves are small today. I wouldn't have brought you out here if I thought you couldn't handle them."

"What about you?"

"I can tread water until I see that you're close enough to shore to stand." He looked back again and slipped his hand out of mine. "Just hang on and let the wave take you in."

He gently pushed himself a couple of feet away so that he was out of the way. I looked behind me and saw what looked like a large wave approaching. My fingers curled around the edge of the bodyboard as I waited for the impact. Before I knew it, I was slowly being pushed back to shore. I held on tightly and fought to keep my balance as the wave got a little bigger with every second.

"You've got it!" I heard James call from behind me.

I smiled as the wave went from what felt like something ready to swallow me whole to practically nothing, and I could feel the sand beneath my feet again. I rolled off of the bodyboard as I came to a slow stop and got to my feet. "That was amazing!" I shouted to him. I watched as he swam close enough to where he could stand but was still chest deep in the water.

"Want to go again?" he called.

"Sure!"

As the day passed, I got better and better at bodyboarding. After the first few tries, he waited out where I started until I swam back out to him with his board. I was amazed at how long he was able to tread water. The flippers he was wearing probably helped a lot with that.

When we were finally tired, we went back to shore and sat on the beach for a while. I watched as he stretched so he wouldn't cramp up later. "Thank you *so* much for today," I said as I dried my hair with one of his beach towels. "I've never done anything like this before, so it was a nice change from my usual routine when I come out here."

He slowly scanned the beach as he stood and did some upper torso twists. "Not a problem. It was nice to have some company for once."

"Jules never comes out here with you?"

"We come out here to unwind every once in a while, but he doesn't come out into the water with me. It's not something he's ever showed interest in."

He flopped down next to me and shoved his flippers into his carrying bag. I looked at his bodyboard and realized that it looked familiar. "How long have you been doing this again?"

"Uh . . . since my junior year in high school, I guess."

"Always at this same spot, by this particular lifeguard tower and everything?"

"I usually start here. Why?"

I watched as he took off his wetsuit jacket. I then noticed that his swim trunks looked familiar, too. It was bothering me that I couldn't figure out where I remembered him from. It was something that I'd been trying to put my finger on ever since we first properly introduced ourselves to each other. "I swear I know you from somewhere," I blurted out.

James folded the wetsuit jacket and sat it to the side with a light sigh. "Do you read the paper or anything?"

"Sometimes, but only when something catches my attention or my parents want me to know something important. Why?"

Without reservation, he began telling me the story about the time he drowned while he was bodyboarding a little while after he graduated from high school. I hung on to every word as he talked about how he had been in the hospital and how worried his parents were that he'd never come out of the coma. His story helped me to remember the article I had read about the incident at the time; the picture of him wearing the same swim trunks and using the same bodyboard stood out in my mind now. It was crazy that I was sitting next to the same person who almost didn't survive such a horrible accident almost two years earlier.

"Who found you?" I asked.

"Some surfers came across my board when they paddled out," he said grimly. "It wouldn't have happened if I had paid attention to the rip current warning posted on the lifeguard tower. I'm more careful when I come out here now."

"But wait—you said you *drowned*," I pointed out.

"I did."

"Shouldn't you be . . . I don't know, dead? Isn't that usually what that means?"

James stared out into the ocean and didn't answer me. I thought about my question and realized that it sounded really insensitive—and childish. "I'm sorry. I didn't mean for it to come out like that. I'm just confused and a little curious."

"The rip current got a hold of me, I panicked, and I ran out of air when I went under. To me, that's drowning. Whether I'm sitting right here talking to you or ended up six feet under in a cemetery, I drowned. I drowned, but I didn't *die*. I mean, I *almost* died. Maybe there's a clinical term for what happened to me. I don't know . . . it's hard to explain," he said.

"We don't have to talk about it anymore if you don't want to." I hugged my legs against my chest and rested my chin on top of my knees.

"It's fine," he insisted. "I find it easier to talk about it than to pretend like it didn't happen."

"Well, if it's any consolation, I'm glad you survived. I would have never gotten the chance to meet you."

"I'm glad too," he said, smiling.

Even though he said it was okay for us to discuss what had happened to him, I found a way to change the subject. I didn't want him dwelling on the past. We ended up talking about school, work, what we were majoring in; it was a basic Q & A session. I got a few laughs out of him when I cracked a couple of jokes, and vice versa. That day at the beach was the longest time we had hung out with each other without the others around us. I was glad that we finally broke through the awkward phase we had been in for so long. As it started to get late, we began to pack up everything we had brought with us so we could head home. I had to be at work the next morning, and he had a few designs to work on for his job.

"So what do you *usually* do when you're out here?" James dusted dry sand from his bodyboard.

"Nothing in particular," I lied.

"You said earlier this is a nice change from your usual routine when you come here, which means, you *do* do something." He gave me a side-glance as he shook sand off of the large beach towel we were sitting on and began to fold it.

"Promise not to laugh?"

"Of course."

"Well, a little after I began dating Jordan in high school, I started coming out here to bury poems and lists in the sand. I thought that maybe if I did it enough that—I don't know—what I wrote down would come to fruition or something." I could feel myself blushing as I listened to myself explain something that he probably wouldn't understand. "That sounds so ridiculous when I say it out loud. I remember the first time I told Alex and Jules what I did when I come out here."

"What'd they say about it?"

We grabbed everything and walked back to his car. "They didn't say anything really . . . which was kind of hard to believe, to be honest."

"They're your friends. What'd you expect them to say?"

"That I'm crazy and then tell Matt and Sam so they could agree, point, and laugh."

"Well, obviously they don't think you're crazy," he chuckled as he unlocked his car. We carefully placed everything into the back seat and then slipped on the clothes we had left in the car so they'd stay dry and sand free while we were out in the water.

"What do *you* think?" I walked around to the passenger side of the car, and he followed. Before I could grab the door handle, he opened the door for me. I thanked him and slid into the warm, dry seat.

"I think that if what you were doing is what kept you from going insane until something better came along, there's nothing wrong with it. My parents told me once that when you put positive thoughts for the things you really want out into the universe, the universe works to make it happen. I think that's how it goes, at least. Regardless, if what you're doing is what's keeping hope alive, that's all that matters, right?"

"Right."

He closed the door for me and got into the car himself. Just as the sky began to change colors, we drove to grab a few snacks from a nearby gas station and then went home. We sat in the car for a few minutes to finish eating what we had bought before I headed upstairs for the night.

"So when's the last time you buried anything at the beach?" He finished the last of his soda and placed the empty can in the cup holder between us.

I thought about it as I opened a package that held a single chocolate chip cookie. "You know, I can't remember. It hasn't really crossed my mind since all of these changes have been occurring. That's probably a good thing."

"I'll say." He sounded relieved. I didn't question it, assuming that he was just tired from our day at the beach.

"Maybe Alex could benefit from going out there and burying her problems after writing them down." I held the cookie in my mouth as I balled up the empty package and shoved it into the plastic bag that held all of the items we had bought from the gas station. I then took a bite out of it and savored the soft, chewy goodness.

"Problems?" James inquired.

"Yeah. We've only been living together for a couple of days, but she's been having a hard time sleeping at night. She keeps calling someone's name in the middle of the night and then ends up in the front room watching TV until she falls back to sleep. It's wearing her out."

"I see. Did you catch the name or anything?"

"I can't be too sure, but I think it starts with an M."

James stare went blank when he heard my answer.

"What's wrong?"

"Nothing. It's just odd, that's all. Has she talked to you about anything that could be going on?"

"I've asked her about it, but she says it's nothing, so I leave her alone. I figure if she wanted to talk about it, she would. Is this the first you've heard about this?"

"It is. But you're right; if she wanted to talk about it, then she would. Are we still on for dinner tomorrow night?"

"We are, and I look forward to it."

He walked me up to the apartment, and we said our good-nights. Alex was sitting in the loveseat watching TV with Raven in her lap. She was dead asleep and didn't even perk her ears to the sound of me coming inside. I locked the door as quietly as I could and placed my keys in the bowl by the door.

"How was the beach?" Alex asked with a yawn.

"I bodyboarded for the first time today," I began excitedly as I jumped onto the couch and had a seat. "I learned a lot about him, too. Did you know he drowned two years ago?"

"I did," she replied drowsily. "He almost didn't come back from that. Most drowning victims don't."

I knew she had worked that morning into the early afternoon, but it looked like she had been working for days on end without an hour of sleep. "Alex, why don't you go to bed early and try to get some rest instead of sitting out here fighting the sandman?"

She looked at her phone when it went off, texted back whomever it was that had sent her a message, and then gently placed Raven on the floor. "I'm fine. I want to hear about your day at the beach."

"I'll tell you all about it tomorrow at work."

I walked her to her room and waited until I was sure she was in bed and not finding her way back to the front room again. *Maybe she's just stressed out with all this planning for our first official group outing*, I thought. *I'm glad that'll be out of the way soon.*

—Chapter 20—

I waited patiently for Alex at a nearby empty lot that was down the street from the diner. I had texted her the night before after I had walked Alora up to their apartment and told her that I needed to talk to her. She agreed to meet up with me on her lunch break. I didn't tell her what I wanted to talk to her about, but I was hoping she'd tell me more about her nightmares since she wasn't talking to Alora or Jules about them. I figured that since we were both near-death experience cases, she'd feel comfortable talking to me about them. When she arrived, I watched as she parked next to me and took off her apron. After she placed it in the passenger seat, she got out and then got into my car.

"Alora told me something yesterday when I brought her home that concerns me," I started. "What's going on with you?"

Alex closed her eyes and rested the back of her head on the headrest. "It's nothing—just some over-the-top dreams. I don't understand why it's such a big deal."

"It's only turning into a big deal because you aren't talking to anyone, especially the people who would understand more than anyone else."

"James, I don't think you or Jules would understand," she groaned. "Your experiences were completely different than mine, especially Jules's. I didn't ask for what's happening, and I wish it had never happened, or even started."

"So something *is* happening," I said sympathetically. "C'mon, Alexia, just tell me what you remember about *any* of the nightmares. I already know about Marie; Alora said you've been calling her name in your sleep. She didn't know the name, per se, but she said she had heard a name that starts with an M. That's more than enough for me to put two and two together."

"I haven't seen Marie since . . . you know. I think I'm just calling out to her for help, but she never shows up. All I've been seeing are flashing pieces of broken images that I can't make out. That's all I can remember."

"And the headaches?"

"I talked to my therapist about those. He said it could possibly be some kind of posttraumatic thing. I don't know. He was using a lot of big medical terms that I couldn't follow, but I have them under control now."

"All of this started before the move, though, right?"

"Yeah, I haven't been doing anything different to cause any of this to start. At first, I figured something around me was changing and that's why they started, but after thinking about it, nothing between me and Jules is going on out of the norm. You and Alora are hitting it off pretty well, and Matt and Sam are fine as usual."

"What about this group outing next week? Is that stressing you out or anything?"

"I'm planning a night out at the annual town fair for the six of us," she laughed. "Granted, it'll be the first time we've all hung out together outside of the dinner we had after the move, but it's not like I'm planning a wedding, you know?"

She was right. With her physical therapy coming to a close at the end of that week, her planning in regard to everyone's getting together for a night of fun, and having all of her classes lined up for the fall, things were going fairly well. The only thing that could have been stressful for her was not being able to move any of her stuff the day she and Alora moved in together.

"None of us have any idea what my supposed special gift is—if I even ended up with anything—and now I'm having these nightmares that are causing me to lose sleep. And . . ." She hesitated for a second and looked out of the passenger window. It was almost as if she wasn't sure she should say what was on her mind.

"What is it, Alex?"

"I do remember *something* from the nightmares—seeing a dark figure. I couldn't make out their face or anything. Something about it is wrong . . . *very* wrong. That's what makes it a nightmare. It's like, my dreams threw up shredded pieces of photos that I can't decipher and tossed in a scary figure that doesn't have good intentions. The only person I've ever thought to call to for help is Marie, but she doesn't show up. So I just force myself awake."

"You've never seen anything or anyone like that before?" I pressed.

"No, and I wish whatever or whoever it is would go away."

Her voice cracked, and she covered her face. The last thing I wanted to do was push her to the point of crying. "I know that coping with what happened has been really hard for you. And I can't tell you why you're having these nightmares or what they could mean. But maybe if you'd just take the time to talk to someone, it may help."

"I don't *want* to talk about it!" she shouted. "I just want to forget."

"You can't forget that you almost died, Alexia," I said sternly. "And you can't pretend like what's happening isn't more than likely a result of it. Stop acting like you can't talk to anyone, or that you shouldn't, or whatever. That makes absolutely no sense. I bet Jules is going crazy because he can't figure out what's wrong. Did you forget that he can sense when something isn't right when it comes to you?"

"How could I *possibly* forget when every time he looks at me, he asks what's wrong because he can see *and* sense there's a problem? And how can I expect either of you to figure out what's wrong when *I* can't even figure out what's wrong? This is tearing me up on the inside," she said hysterically.

"Okay, okay, calm down," I coaxed. "Am I the only one you've told about this figure you've been seeing?"

"Yeah," she sniffled. "And don't you *dare* tell Jules," she threatened. "He'll run himself into the ground trying to solve a mystery that isn't his to worry about. You know that as much as I do."

"I don't think we should keep this from him," I admitted.

"This is *really* important, James." She grabbed my hand and squeezed it. "The last thing I'd want you to do is lie to your best friend, but I'm asking that you *please* keep this between us until I'm ready to talk to him about it. From there, the three of us can try and put the pieces together. *Please.*"

Her eyes were pleading for me to agree. I sighed and squeezed the bridge of my nose with the hand that she wasn't already holding. "Okay . . . but o*nly* if you promise to report anything new to me. I won't hold up my end of the bargain if you refuse to tell me what's going on."

"Yes, I promise." She gave my hand an extra squeeze to seal the deal and then let out a huge sigh of relief. "I feel *so* much better since I've talked to someone about this."

"Yeah, well, I wish the feeling were mutual," I mumbled.

"I'd better get back to the diner. Thanks again, James."

"No problem."

No good can come from this, I thought.

—Chapter 21—

I skipped down the three flights of stairs that led to our apartment with an empty trash bag in tow, letting my brightly colored sundress flow behind me. The weather was perfect for the upcoming festivities at the town fair that evening. I had offered to drive Alex, James, and Jules there to meet up with Matt and Sam, so I wanted to make sure my car was as clean as it possibly could be before everyone got inside of it. I only had a few minutes before James and Jules would arrive, so I had to be quick about it.

First, I cleaned out the back of the car. It had over ten empty candy wrappers strewn all over the floor and the seats. "I'm surprised I don't have ants in here," I snickered. I then moved to the trunk, where I took out the towel I had used to dry Raven off the last time I took her to the beach so it could be washed. From there, I started to clean up the little bit of trash that was in the front of the car. When I got to the middle console, I ran across the black plastic sheet that the stranger had given to me the night I had went to the beach to clear my head. I was about to throw it away when I noticed that something was in it. I carefully pulled out the sheet of paper that was inside; my eyes widened as what was on it became more visible.

"Wow," I gasped.

It was a sketch of me and Raven playing fetch on the beach. The colors were so vibrant, and the detail was amazing. I peeked inside the plastic sheet to see if there was anything else inside, but the drawing was all there was. After making sure the car was clean, I quickly made my way back up to the apartment so I could show Alex.

"Alex!" I called as I walked in. I dropped the bag of trash into the trash can in the kitchen and took a seat at the dining room table. "Alex, come look at this!"

She came out of her room with Raven right behind her. She was putting on a pair of earrings that matched her summer romper. "What is it?"

"Look at what I found in the car while I was cleaning it out." I held it up to her so she could take a look at it. Her eyes widened the same way mine had when I first looked at it.

"It's beautiful," she gasped. "You said you found that in your car?"

"Yeah," I said as I ran my finger lightly across some of the colors. "Some guy gave it to me the night I went to the beach after the whole money incident."

"Really? Why didn't you tell me about that when I asked you if anything out of the norm had happened after your job interview?"

"I didn't think it was something I needed to tell you. Besides, by then I had completely forgotten that this was in my car. Well, I didn't know what *it* was because it was in some plastic sheet that was blacked out—"

"It's a black-lined page protector," Alex corrected.

"Well, if you want to be technical about it," I shrugged.

A knock at the front door interrupted our conversation. I carefully dropped the drawing back into the page protector and went to answer the door. Alex went back into her room so she could finish getting ready. Jules walked in, but James wasn't with him. "You're missing someone," I laughed as I gave him a hug.

"He shouldn't be long." Jules took a seat at the dining room table as I closed the front door. We had told him to dress comfortably since it was his first time going to the town fair, so he went with a pair of jeans, clean sneakers, and a polo shirt.

"Alex will be out in a minute. I'll be right back." I took the drawing into my room and placed it on my dresser after taking one last peek at it. I saw something smudged down in the lower right-hand corner, but I couldn't make out what it was. I figured I'd take a closer look at it when we got home that evening and went back out to the front room. I found James standing at the front door in a pair of khaki cargo shorts, a V-neck T-shirt, and a pair of sneakers. He was holding a huge item wrapped in brown paper.

"What's that?" I asked with a raised brow.

"It's a little something to commemorate your brand new start." He held it out so I could take it from him.

"Aw." I walked up to him and gently took it out of his hands. I had to set it down because it had a bit of weight to it.

"I thought this would be a nice apartment-warming gift. It took me some time to get it ready, so I hope you like it. Sorry it's a little late and all."

James and Jules watched in silence as I slowly unwrapped it. Alex stepped out into the hallway from her room so she could watch as well. When all the paper was finally off, I found myself staring at the pastel drawing that he had used for his final art appreciation grade. On the bottom of the frame, "Pick-up Stix" was engraved into it with our move-in date and his initials.

"Well, that was nice of you, James." Alex walked over to Jules so she could sit next to him while putting on her sandals.

"Do we have enough time to hang it?" I asked her.

"Sure."

"I brought some nails so it can be mounted in your bedroom." James dug into his shorts pocket and showed them to us. "You guys have a hammer?"

"There should be one in here," I said as I led him down the hall to the small laundry room.

He dug through Alex's overflowing toolbox that her father had given her until he found a small hammer. I then led him into my room and showed him the perfect spot to hang it. It was between two windows that faced the bedroom door. "That way I will see it every time I walk in," I explained.

I sat on the end of my bed and watched him mount the picture on the wall. After making sure it was sturdy, he took a step back and took a long look at it. "Does it look crooked or anything?"

I got up and stood next to him so I could see it better. "Hmm . . . it looks straight to me. Alex may have a level if you want to double check."

"I trust your judgment." He looked around the room and spotted the page protector on my dresser. "What's that?"

"Oh, it's this really nice sketch of me and Raven at the beach. Some guy gave it to me one night when I was out there weeks ago."

"Can I see it?"

"Sure." I grabbed it and slowly pulled the paper out. I gazed at it as if it were my first time seeing it. "Gorgeous, right?"

He stared at it and smiled. "It is. And you have *no* idea who the artist was?"

"There's a smudge down at the bottom that I tried to make out, but I figured I'd take a better look at it when I got home tonight." I pointed to what I was talking about, and he took it from me.

James gave it a couple of brisk rubs and pressed it between his thumb and index finger. "Can you read it now?"

I took it back from him and was speechless. Not believing what I was seeing at first, I walked over to the new piece of artwork hanging on my wall to compare the initials. The "JS" matched perfectly. "That was *you* that night?"

"Yup."

I immediately felt embarrassed. "I called you a maniac hermit and accused you of keeping women hostage in your hermit tent."

James laughed loudly. "I took no offense at that, trust me. You had every reason to assume that I was some weirdo prowling on females at the beach."

"That hoodie didn't help you any," I said, smirking.

"I was nervous, and that was a poor move on my part. I actually thought it ruined my chances to get to know you."

"It almost did." I took the picture and stuck it in the corner of the dresser mirror. "Now I'm *really* glad you survived that drowning incident."

"Ah, geez," he gushed as he gave me a hug. "Let's not get too sentimental. You'll make me blush," he joked.

We both walked out to the front room and found Alex and Jules playing with Raven in the middle of the room. She immediately ran to me when she saw me and began jumping all over me. "Who's a good girl? You're a good girl!" I ruffled her fur between her ears, and she began whining happily. Afterward, she crawled under her favorite chair, curled up, and got ready to fall asleep. She was getting better at knowing when we were going out and knew the routine.

"You guys ready?" Jules got to his feet and helped Alex to hers.

"The real question is, are *you* ready?" James asked. "This will be the first time you've attended our annual town fair."

"It can't be anything out of the ordinary, right? There'll be a few rides, a Ferris wheel, games, a few animals there to be judged—"

The three of us looked at one another and shook our heads as we suppressed our laughter.

"What? Am I missing something?"

I took James by the hand and led him to the front door. After I grabbed my keys from the bowl, I quickly slipped on my sandals. "Those West Coast fairs must be kiddie parks in comparison to what we have here every year."

"Clearly," Alex snorted as they followed us out of the apartment. She took a moment to text Matt and Sam that we were on our way and made sure the door was locked behind us. Once we were all settled in the car, I drove us to our destination. We couldn't wait to see what the night had in store for us.

—Chapter 22—

Light from bright, colorful lamps danced across the faces of everyone in the car as I pulled into a parking space close to the fair entrance. Jules stared out of the window in awe as we got ourselves together to meet up with Matt and Sam. They were already inside waiting for us.

"*This* is a fair?" Jules gawked as we all got out of the car.

Alex laughed. "Pretty huge, huh?"

"I'll say. It looks like someone took half of a theme park and dropped it in the middle of a fairground. This is amazing!" I could hear the excitement in his voice as he took in the sight in front of him. "I've never been to a fair this big. It's overwhelming."

"Take a deep breath, tiger," I remarked as I locked the car. "We wouldn't want you to pass out from all the excitement."

The annual town fair was something everyone looked forward to every year. When it had first come to town, it was much smaller, a typical-sized fair. But it had gotten a lot of business since not a lot happened in the area, so each year, ever since I could remember, it grew bigger and bigger. It got so big, in fact, that it was moved from a vacant parking lot to a fairground so that all of the games and rides would fit. There were at least two oversized wooden roller coasters, a bunch of different-sized fun houses, two large Ferris wheels, a section for the younger children, countless food and game booths, animal petting corrals—if you named an attraction that could possibly be at a fair, it was there. Alex was able to grab a few flyers at the diner one evening that advertised discounted "hopper bands" with the purchase of a regular admission ticket, which allowed the wearer to hop to the front of the line for every ride in the park at least once. She gave Matt and Sam theirs in advance so they wouldn't miss out on the deal and made sure she had enough for the four of us for when we got there.

"Where are Matt and Sam, exactly?" James asked Alex.

"I'll find out." She pulled her phone out of one of her pockets and quickly composed a text.

"We should hurry before the ticket line gets any longer." He stood by me as we waited for Alex to receive a response from Matt or Sam.

"We got here in enough time to ride everything at least once, so what's the rush? We've been here a million times. Nothing has changed," I pointed out as I brushed down my sundress.

"No, James is right. We may have all evening to ride everything and whatnot, but we *don't* have all evening to snag a hopper band for each of us. We should get in line before they're all sold out," Alex suggested as she herded the three of us closer to the front entrance.

I scanned the row of ticket booths as we approached and tried to find one with a line moving relatively fast. "Over there." I pointed to one at the very end of the row, and we quickly walked over to it. Once we were in line, I placed my hand out in front of everyone. "I'll get the tickets. You guys stand over by the entry gate so no one thinks you're in line. It should only take me a couple of minutes to get everything we need."

Alex gave me the money I had given her the week before to hold for me along with the money for her and Jules. James looked at me in confusion when I didn't try to collect anything from him.

"What about my ticket?" he asked me curiously.

"It's my treat."

Alex ushered them away to a nearby bench before he could object. "Don't forget the hopper bands," she reminded me.

I nodded as I crept closer to the ticket window. As I looked ahead, I noticed that almost every person was walking away from the booth with at least three hopper bands. I hoped that by the time I got there, enough bands would be left for me to purchase four. I finally made it to the front of the line and eagerly waited to be acknowledged so I could approach the window.

"How many?" The cashier brought her face close to the speaker box that enabled her to talk to customers through the thick glass. She didn't look as if she wanted to be there—that or she was uncomfortable from baking in the warm, small, stuffy booth she had to work in while wearing an oversized, multicolored polo work shirt. Her name tag, which read "Betty," was pinned crookedly to striped suspenders.

I unfolded the money and flyers to obtain the hopper band discount, walked up to the booth, and slid everything into the silver tray that went under the window. "Four adult tickets, and four hopper bands please," I requested as I watched the cashier pull everything into the little booth.

Betty took her time counting the cash and made sure all of the bills were facing the same way as I stood and waited patiently. A bead of sweat rolled down her nose and dripped onto the counter. She finally finished counting the money, put it in the cash drawer, threw away the flyers after inspecting them, and slid four tickets to me under the window. She then began to dig through the drawer that I assumed housed the hopper bands. She placed two into the silver tray and then slowly opened other drawers as she searched for two more. I began to get anxious. *Please let there be two more,* I thought. If she didn't have any left, two of us would have to miss out on the line hopping.

Finally, she located two bands. She placed them with the first two she had found and slid them under the window. "Lucky you. You got the last four I had. Enjoy your evening." She looked past me and signaled for the next customer to step up as she placed an "Out of Hopper Bands" sign against the window. I heard sighs and curses of disappointment as I happily walked toward Alex and the guys. They each took a ticket from me and placed the bands on their wrists. Moments later, we were inside the fair. We let Jules stand and take a good look at everything again before we went to meet up with Matt and Sam.

"I wonder if his head is going to explode," Alex whispered to me and James as we watched Jules's eyes glaze over.

"I really do think his mind is melting a little at the sight at all of this," James laughed. "You okay, buddy?"

"I'm usually not taken aback by things like this, but I'm at a loss for words." Jules still sounded shocked at the size of the fair.

"Come on. Let's find the rest of our party before they think we got lost . . . and before this guy forgets how to walk and talk. They're waiting by one of the small petting zoos on the other side of the grounds." Alex took Jules by the arm and slowly started to walk; I did the same with James. At first, we walked around so Jules could get an idea of what rides we planned on getting on that night. When we finally met up with Matt and Sam, we all decided that we should start with the small water rides to cool down from the summer heat. We figured that if we got completely drenched first, we could dry off on one of the roller coasters or swing rides located on the other side of the kiddie area. After that, we'd sit and eat and then play a few games.

We finished all of the water rides in under an hour. I was the first to get wet from one of the large drops we encountered at the very beginning of the last one we rode. James, Jules, and Matt laughed at me only to end up getting wet at some of the most random moments. Alex and Sam, on the other hand, managed to keep dry the entire time. That didn't surprise me; over all the years we had been going to the fair since we were kids, they had always managed to avoid getting wet.

"That was fun," James said as he wrung some water out from the end of his shirt. "I just wish I hadn't worn my good sneakers tonight, though. They're soaked from the inside out."

"I'm sure they'll get dry on one of the swing rides," Sam pointed out.

"I'm ready to get on one of those right now. Let's make our way to that side of the fair before I get hungry." Jules patted his wet shirt against his stomach, creating a quiet splat.

"Actually, could we switch up the game plan and eat now?" Alex said as she slowed down.

"Maybe we should." Matt stopped walking and took a close look at her. "You look a little pale. You didn't swallow any of that nasty water from those rides, did you?"

Alex smiled faintly. "Look at me, Matt. Not a single drop of water touched me the entire time," she pointed out proudly.

"She's probably just exhausted. She hasn't been getting much sleep lately," I reported.

"No, that's not it. I've been sleeping better," she said defensively.

"Well, then maybe you haven't caught up on all the sleep you've lost," James said. "We've got all night, and there's no point in going back and forth about how pale you look or how much sleep you haven't gotten. You're okay with taking a break, right, Jules? I promise you'll get your money's worth before we leave here tonight." James got on his tippy toes and scanned the fair to try and find the nearest food booth.

"That's fine. I'd rather take a break than risk Alex passing out or something. They've got funnel cakes, right? It's been a while since I've had one."

"Of course they have funnel cakes, you weirdo. It's a fair." Sam shook her head and motioned for us to follow her. "We passed by a decent-looking food booth when we first got here. It's this way."

We followed Sam and got settled at one of the large wooden picnic tables closer to the front of the fair. Alex rested her head on the tabletop while she waited for Jules to bring their food over. Matt and James had gone with him so they could get our food as well. I stayed behind with Sam so I could keep an eye on Alex.

"How long has she been like this?" Sam whispered.

"I can't readily say," I admitted. "It *was* worse, but she was telling the truth when she said she's been sleeping better. I wish she'd just tell me what's wrong."

"There's nothing going on between her and Jules, right?"

"If there is, I can't tell. I highly doubt it, though."

"Well look who's here," we heard.

We both looked up and saw Jordan and a few of his friends standing at the end of the table. I looked over at Alex to see if she had noticed that he was there, but she was sound asleep. How she was able to get any kind of rest with all of the noise going on around her was beyond me, but I wasn't going to allow Jordan to take that moment of peace away from her.

"Go away, Jordan," Sam ordered.

"Hello to you too, Samantha," he scoffed.

"Seriously, Jordan, *go away*," I said sternly. "We don't have the time or the patience to deal with your shenanigans tonight. Go cause trouble with your goon squad somewhere else."

"Well, look who decided to grow a voice all of the sudden," Jordan mocked. His friends laughed as they looked on.

I looked over to the food booth and saw that the guys' backs were to us. *Better now than never*, I thought. "Can I talk to you for a second?" I said with a false smile.

By the look on Jordan's face, I could tell I had caught him by surprise. "Sure."

I got up from the table, brushed down my sundress, and led him over to a small area where a group of garbage cans were. When I knew I wasn't in earshot of Alex or Sam, I spoke. "Remember when you said that you didn't think I understood how a breakup works?" I narrowed my eyes and crossed my arms.

"What's that got to do with anything?"

"The thing is, I don't think *you* understand how it works. The point is to move on and leave the other person alone—especially if things didn't end on good terms. And we, obviously, didn't end on good terms. So why can't you leave me the *hell* alone?" I raised my voice only a little but enough to show that I was serious. "This whole thing that you're doing? It's childish. Yeah, I was torn up about what happened and all in the beginning, but I'm not magically appearing at random locations you're at and harassing *you*."

"You probably would if you weren't trying so hard to occupy your spare time with your clan of misfit friends and what I'm assuming is your new boy toy," he snickered.

"Don't flatter yourself." I looked past him to make sure our food hadn't arrived yet. Alex was still taking her cat nap, and it looked as though Sam was keeping a lookout as best she could. Jordan's friends were laughing amongst themselves as they waited for him to rejoin them. "Do me a favor, and stop bothering me. Obviously, I've moved on. You should too."

I pushed past him to make my way back to the table, but I didn't get too far before he grabbed me by the arm. I gave him a look that caused his eyes to widen and loosen his grip. "Take your group of friends and get away from our table," I growled.

We stared each other down for a brief moment before he called to his group and stormed away without saying another word. When they were all out of sight, I walked back to our table just as the guys brought the food over. Sam looked at me, and I gave a slight nod to let her know everything was fine. Jules tapped Alex on her shoulder, and she woke up.

"Is your battery charged from that power nap?" He handed her a bottle of water and some fries.

"It is, actually," she said after taking a drink and a bite of a few of the fries. "I should be fine after I eat."

James brought over a hamburger for me and a cup of soda for us to share. He had bought himself a hot dog to go along with everything, and Matt had grabbed a couple of slices of pizza and a soda for him and Sam. Out of nowhere, a white cloud of smoke filled the air, and Jules began coughing uncontrollably.

Alex started laughing hysterically as she handed him her bottle of water. "I've told you about chewing funnel cakes and not inhaling them. That's what you get."

Once Jules was able to get down some water to stop coughing, he laughed as well. "You know I get ahead of myself with these things."

"How do you like the fair so far?" Matt asked him between bites.

"I'm really enjoying myself. We should definitely do things like this as a group more often." Jules pulled a couple of pieces of funnel cake off of the larger part and took his time eating it this time so he wouldn't choke on the powdered sugar.

"This *is* nice," Sam agreed. "Once school starts and we've got our schedules lined up, it'll be easier to plan group outings once or twice a week . . . or month," she laughed, "whichever is easier."

I spaced out as I thought about how I had confronted Jordan for the first time ever without the help of Alex, James, or Jules. I was so proud of myself that I was ready to burst at the seams. I took a bite of my burger and listened to everyone talk about how excited they were about school being back in session soon and the different activities we could do together throughout the year. *I can't wait to see how the rest of the night turns out.* I smiled at James as he took a sip of soda and then offered me some. *Hopefully that talk I had with Jordan was enough to get rid of him for good this time.*

—Chapter 23—

"I probably shouldn't go in with you guys," Alex said as she took a nervous step back away from us.

The six of us were standing in front of one of the larger fun houses there. There were five floors filled with anything and everything a fun house could possibly have inside of it. The first two floors were outside, while the last three were inside. Alex hadn't said anything about not wanting to participate with us until we actually got to it. She was fine with the water rides, roller coasters, swing ride, and the Ferris wheel, but she was ready to back out as we were bringing our night to a close.

"Oh, come on, Alex," Sam pressured her. "I'm sure it won't be that bad."

"Think of all the stuff in there that could reset my physical therapy, though. Shifting floors, getting spooked and tripping while running away from something, that weird tube thing that spins—I should *really* sit this one out."

"She's right," I agreed. "I want her to come in with us but not if it'll be unsafe for her."

"We'll keep her entertained until you two get back. Maybe we can hit up a few game booths close by until you guys get out," Jules suggested.

The guys had gone through one of the other fun houses earlier that evening together while we had waited outside for them. It was their turn to wait for us; it just sucked that Alex was opting to sit out.

"We shouldn't be long," Sam promised as she headed to the spiral staircase that led up to the fifth floor of the fun house.

"I'll try to win you something," James gave me a gentle push in the same direction Sam had gone. "Have fun."

While making our ascent, I watched as the rest of our group slowly walked away toward a small area where there were some games that offered fairly large prizes. It was nice to be able to see exactly where they were, but moments later, they wandered farther away and were out of sight.

"Don't worry. We'll find them if they wander farther than we expected." Sam grabbed my hand so we could speed up. Once we were at the top of the staircase, we entered a small, winding hallway that led out to the first walkway with what looked like a normal floor. The second we both stepped on it, it jerked forward and then back again, and then it was still. We looked at each other wide eyed and then started laughing hysterically.

"I wasn't expecting that," I said as I caught my breath. "You think the entire way is like this?"

"I don't know, but we're about to find out," Sam said mischievously.

We took our time enjoying the fifth floor. Other people made their way past us so they could get to the bottom as quickly as possible. We played on some of the more fun shifting floor panels and caused short bursts of air to blow through our hair from the wall as we finally got to the end of the walkway. The fourth floor was more like a bounce house. I had a difficult time keeping my balance at first, but after a moment or two of having spaghetti legs, we jumped around until we were out of breath.

When we were finished there, we stood at the end of the walkway before making our way down to the third floor.

"Alex is missing out on some fun," Sam panted. "Hopefully next year she'll be able to come into one of these with us."

"I'm sure she'll be able to." I adjusted my sundress and waited until Sam was ready to go. I tensed up when I heard people shrieking at the top of their lungs from below us. "Sounds promising," I said with a raised brow.

"C'mon, let's see what the fuss is about." Sam led the way as we eagerly went down to the third floor. Once there, we stood for a moment and looked at what was ahead of us. The room was much larger than we had anticipated it to be. Bright lights were shining through long pieces of what looked to be heavy curtain that was draped around the ceiling and between walls of mirrors. The floors looked like they were mirrors as well. "You think it's real glass?" Sam carefully stepped on the floor and looked around.

"Uh—I would hope the floor isn't. Maybe the walls are, but if *everything* around us were made of glass, that'd be dangerous, I think."

"Well, what're we waiting for? Let's go!" Sam ran ahead and went down one of the small hallways that split and went into two different directions.

"Sam, wait!"

I slowly walked in the same direction that she had gone with my hand sliding across the glass panels on my left. As I did, I discovered that it split again. "Samantha!" I called. I heard another group of people giggling as I tried to decide whether to go left or right. I tripped over an extension cord that powered a couple of the lights hanging overhead. "That can't be safe," I mumbled as I went down the hallway to the right. It began to get confusing because my reflection and the reflection of the hot lights above me were bouncing all over the place. I got frustrated when I hit a dead end. "Really? A *maze* of mirrors? It'll take me forever to get out of here," I groaned.

I backtracked to where I thought I had first gone down the right hallway but immediately realized that I was turned around. It looked like I was coming across a new split in the hallway, and I had to choose a different direction like before. "Sam! I think I'm lost! Where are you?" I waited to hear a response from her, but I didn't get one. "I'm going to wring her neck when I get out of here," I said to myself. I quickly walked down the left hallway in hopes that it'd lead back to the entrance of the third floor. Halfway down, I came face to face with Jordan and his friends. "You've *got* to be kidding me."

"Lost?" Jordan said with a mischievous grin.

"Actually, I am," I admitted. "If you know the way out and could help me, then great. If you're only here to cause trouble, then get out of my way, and I'll find my own way out." I stepped to the side, and they all blocked me. I tried again the other way, and they stepped to that side as well. I was getting more irritated the longer I was forced to stand there and play their stupid game. "Jordan, *move*. Everyone is probably waiting for me outside," I pleaded.

"Why don't you text Alexia or your boyfriend so they can swoop in and save you like always?" He reached into my sundress pocket and took my phone out of it.

"Hey!" I tried to snatch it back from him, but he had a firm grip on it.

He dropped the phone onto the ground and then stomped on it. "Oops."

"Have you lost your mind?" I shouted. "That was totally uncalled for!"

"I bought you that too, remember?" He stomped on it again without hesitation, watching as the insides of it scattered all over the place and cracked the floor.

When he went to stomp on it a third time, I slapped him clean across his face as hard as I possibly could and then shoved him into his group of friends. I didn't stick around to see what his obvious reaction would be; I made a run for it in the direction I had come from when I was trying to find my way back to the entrance of the maze.

"Get back here!" I heard him holler.

Heavy footsteps echoed around me as I tried to find my way out of the maze of mirrors. When I came back to the split in the hallway, I made sure I didn't trip on the extension cord and went left instead of right. I then went down the right hallway when it split again and then swung another left. In the distance, I saw the glow of the sign that read "To Second Floor." Before I could head toward it as fast as I could, I heard glass shatter behind me and saw two of the overhead lights crash into each other, which caused one of them to fall from the ceiling and the other to go out. The reflection of the sparks from the lights lit up in all of the mirrors as the clashing noise slowly stopped echoing throughout the third floor. Before I knew it, Jordan's friends were running past me to the exit, but he wasn't with them. I hesitated for a second to see if he'd shortly follow, but he didn't. *The exit is right there*, I thought. *If he hurt himself, that's his own fault.* Just as I turned away to leave, I smelled smoke.

I quickly walked back the way I had come, hoping that I wouldn't come across Jordan in *any* way, shape, or form. The smoke was getting thicker, and the room was starting to turn a bright orange. My heart sank when I turned the corner and saw Jordan lying in a pile of broken glass. He was out cold. He had tripped over the same extension cord I had tripped over when I first entered the maze, only he had tripped on it so badly that he had fallen head first into one of the mirrored walls. That was the reason the two connected overhead lights had collided and one had come crashing down. He was lucky it didn't fall *on* him. A small fire from the heat of the light that fell started on one of the curtains that was between the mirror panels and was getting bigger by the minute. I tried to move the mirror pane in an effort to put it out before it spread, but it wouldn't budge.

"Someone help!" I shouted. "Fire!" I grabbed Jordan's arm, hoping it'd be easy to pull him across the mirrored floor to the exit, but I couldn't move him. Bulbs from the other lights above us were starting to pop from overheating, which caused glass shards to go flying through the air. "Jordan, wake up!" I shook him, hoping he'd come to so we could get out of there, but he didn't even flinch. "Why won't you wake up!" I shouted at the top of my lungs. By then, the air was thick with smoke, so I got as low to the floor as I possibly could and stayed close to him. I took a few deep breaths of what would probably be the last bit of fresh air I would get until I made it outside and worked to pull him again. This time, he began to budge a little. I moved some of the broken glass from around him and tugged harder. I managed to get him down one of the hallways that led to the exit as I hacked and coughed. I tried to breathe normally, but it was becoming increasingly difficult. My eyes were burning and tearing from the thick smoke that was engulfing us as the fire grew. "I've got to get us out of here," I grunted as I gave his arm another tug.

The fire alarm began to ring throughout the fun house. By the time I got to the beginning of the last hallway, I was exhausted. I squinted through the tears welled up in my eyes and couldn't even see the exit sign anymore. I panicked. "Help! There are people trapped in here!" I tried to scream, but my voice was raspy from all of the smoke I had inhaled. My attention was directed to a loud creaking that came from the ceiling above us. I watched as some of it fell and landed on Jordan's right leg. He sat up, screamed in pain, and grabbed his thigh as he tried to pull his leg out from under the rubble.

"Hang on," I coughed as I reached over and tried to push it off. I pulled my hands back after touching the beam when it burned the palm of my right hand. Movement from the hallway I had dragged Jordan from caught my attention through the smoke. "Hello?"

I watched as the reflection of a little girl wearing a white dress appeared in all of the mirrors that led up to where we were. She was holding a small red fire truck and just stared at the both of us.

"We need help!"

She continued to stare but didn't move a muscle.

Everything around me started to get blurry as I coughed profusely. I could barely see the little girl anymore as everything around me began to close in. Jordan's screams began to fade, and I felt myself giving in to what felt like nothingness. I heard what sounded like someone calling my name, but I was too tired to try and call back. Another coughing fit came over me as I felt like I was beginning to float.

"It's okay, Alora. I've got you. Everything will be okay," I heard someone whisper. I heard glass shattering around me as I started moving toward a bright light.

I tried to speak, but I was so light-headed from the smoke that I blacked out.

—Chapter 24—

I ran my fingers over the stitching of the oversized softball before throwing it at the pyramid of milk bottles.

"You know this game is rigged, right?" Jules whispered in my right ear.

"You'll *never* knock them all over," Matt hissed in my left ear.

"Guys! James didn't mess with either of you when it was your turn. Give him some room to breathe! Geez," Alex broke in.

Both Jules and Matt chuckled as they took a few steps back from me. I had my eye on a large stuffed bear I wanted to win for Alora so I could give it to her when she came out of the fun house. Jules had managed to win Alex a prize, and Matt had won something for Sam. I was still trying to win something, but I was losing at every game I tried. We had ended up back at the front of the fair as we looked for a game that we thought I'd have no trouble winning. After taking a deep breath, I threw the softball as hard as I could, but I only knocked two of the three bottles off of the wooden podium.

"Oh, come on!" I threw my hands up into the air in defeat.

"Maybe we should try a different kind of game," Jules suggested. "You keep getting pulled into these types, and you lose every time."

"He gave them all a good shot, though," Matt said in my defense.

It was the fourth game that I had spent money on, and I couldn't even win a small stuffed animal. I checked my pockets and realized that I was out of money. "I can't, guys. I'm out of cash for the night. I probably should have paced myself."

"Here's a little something for being a good sport." The booth operator handed me what looked like the smallest stuffed giraffe I'd ever seen.

"Thanks," I said in disappointment.

"I'm sure she'll like it, James," Alex said in an effort to reassure me.

"Not when she sees what these two won for you and Sam."

Alex was toting around an oversized stuffed dog Jules had won that was half her size. Matt was holding a long, bean-stuffed snake for Sam.

"It's the thought that counts." Jules patted me on the shoulder as the four of us made our way to a small, wooden table.

"Well, maybe if the both of you hadn't been in my ear, I *would* have knocked all the milk bottles over." I flopped down on the bench and dropped the stuffed giraffe on the table.

"You know we were just messing with you. You *also* know that these games are rigged. You should have taken a chance at the Strongman Sledgehammer game. You would have won a prize regardless, even if you didn't ring the bell at the top." Matt sat next to me and readjusted the stuffed snake he had wrapped around him so it wouldn't drag on the ground.

"Speaking of prize, how's that keepsake box repair coming along?" Alex asked as she and Jules took a seat across from us.

"It's almost finished. I just have to put some finishing touches on it, and then I'll be able to give it back to her."

We talked for a while as we waited on Alora and Sam to find us. We all checked our phones to see if they had texted any of us to find out where we were, but we hadn't gotten anything.

"It didn't take us this long to get out of the fun house we went into," Matt pointed out. "I wonder what's taking them so long."

"Maybe there were a lot of people going through it," Alex suggested.

"I don't think so. When we left them, there weren't a lot of people going in or coming out. If it's taking them this long, it's because there are five floors in that stupid thing." I checked my phone again and placed it on the table.

"We'll give them a few more minutes," Alex said. "If we don't hear anything from them, we should probably head back over there. It's starting to get late." She yawned.

No sooner had Alex said that than Sam found us. She sat next to Matt and squeezed the stuffed snake. "This is the biggest prize you've ever won for me," she gushed.

"Where's Alora?" I asked her.

"She's still in the fun house. I think she may have gotten turned around on the third floor; it's a mirror maze. She's going to kill me when she finally gets out because I left her behind."

"Nice one, Sam," Matt said flatly.

"She'll be okay," Sam promised. "Once she figures it out, it's just two more floors and then she'll be out of there."

"How long do you think it'll take her?" Jules asked.

"It shouldn't take her much longer. A few other people were passing through, so if she can't find her way out, I'm sure she'll ask someone for help." Sam gave her stuffed snake another squeeze and bopped Matt on the nose with it.

We watched a few other groups of people pass us holding sticks of cotton candy as they made their way back to the parking lot. Small children were chatting a million miles a minute as they shoved their small bags of goldfish in each other's faces that they won at one of the game booths. *Even a pet goldfish is better than this nothing of a stuffed toy*, I thought to myself.

"I need a drink," Alex announced. She handed the oversized stuffed dog to Jules, and he took it. "I'm going to go grab some water. Do any of you want anything?"

"I could go for a snack or something. I'll come with you so I can take a look at the menu." I handed the small giraffe to Matt. "Make sure no one tries to take it," I said overdramatically.

We stood in a short line at a snack booth. Alex dug into one of her pockets and pulled out a ten dollar bill. While reading the menu to decide on what I wanted, our attention was directed to some kids who were crying at another snack booth a few feet away. Apparently, they were upset that their parents wouldn't pay $3.50 for a large bag of blue cotton candy. I watched as the little girl fell to the ground and began to throw a huge temper tantrum. Her younger brother was hitting his father's legs and then proceeded to pull at their mother's skirt. Seconds later, the parents broke down and got them *each* a bag.

"Spoiled brats," Alex mumbled.

I silently agreed with her. I never did that when I was their age. If I wanted something from my parents and I got it, then fine. If I didn't, I didn't. If I even thought about trying to throw a temper tantrum, I knew I would have gotten a quick slap to the butt. That would have ended it before it started.

Alex paid for a small bag of popcorn for me and a bottle of water for her. We stepped up to a small condiment table so I could add butter and salt and so that she could open the water and throw the cap away.

"Thanks again for not telling Jules about what we talked about last week." She took a large drink from the bottle until it was half empty.

"It hasn't been easy keeping this secret from him." I shook some extra salt into the popcorn bag, closed it, and began to shake it to spread it around. "Alora made a pretty good suggestion, though, if she hasn't already told you."

"Which was?"

"Write down what's bothering you so it'll take your mind off of it for a while. Maybe you should get a journal to log your nightmares in or something. It may help jog your memory. That way, when you piece things together, you can tell us what you've been seeing." I took a handful of popcorn and shoved it in my mouth when I was finished shaking the bag. "I mean, I'm sure you want to forget, but this recurring dream may be a message or something. You know what I mean?"

I looked at Alex and saw that her face was pale. She was staring off into the distance, and it looked like she wasn't breathing. "Alex?"

She dropped her bottle of water and continued staring. Then, without warning, she turned to me and grabbed my arm. I dropped my popcorn when she broke into a run and began pulling me along behind her. "Alex, what's wrong?"

"It's Alora," she panted as she started to run faster.

She let go of my arm as I began running at the same speed as her without needing her guidance. "Guys! Something's wrong!" I shouted as we ran past the table our group was sitting at. Jules, Matt, and Sam left the prizes behind as they got to their feet and quickly followed behind us. The five of us weaved in and out of the sea of people who were waiting in line for rides or just watching rides go by. Suddenly, we were all knocked to the ground by a group of guys running at the same rate of speed in the opposite direction.

"Watch where you're going," Jules said as he grabbed Alex by the arm and helped her get back on her feet.

Matt and Sam helped me to mine. "Hey, you're the guys who were with Jordan earlier. Where's your ringleader?" Sam panted.

They all looked at one another as they got to their feet and started running again without answering Sam. We all jumped at the sound of an ear-piercing scream that came from ahead of us. People began running in the direction of the fun house Alora was in.

"We're running out of time!" Alex snatched her arm from Jules's hand and began running full speed again toward the fun house.

I looked up into the sky and saw black smoke rising. "No," I gasped, "this can't be happening . . ."

Confusion and fear were in the air when we reached the front of the fun house. Workers were telling people to stand back; the sound of the fire alarm rang loudly as we stood and looked on in shock and disbelief. Alex turned to me after staring for a moment, and she pulled me close to her face so no one else could hear her. "I see her," she said, her voice trembling.

"You see *who*?"

"Marie. We have to get to Alora; there isn't much time."

I looked back and saw the panic in Jules's and Matt's eyes. Sam was sitting on the ground crying. "I shouldn't have left her behind," she kept repeating out loud. "If something happens to her, it'll be my fault."

I walked over to her and squatted down so that I could look her in the eye. "Nothing will happen to her, I promise." After Matt sat next to Sam so he could try to calm her down, I rose to my feet and pulled Jules over to Alex. "We're going in for Alora," I said to her bluntly.

"Okay. C'mon, I'll lead the way," she said.

"Not me and you—me and Jules."

Her eyes got wide, and then she broke into a fit of rage. "You're *not* taking him in there with you. You can't!" she shouted as she grabbed my shirt.

"Alexia, let *go* of me!"

Jules grabbed her and pulled her off of me. I took a step back from her; he held her in case she tried to lunge at me again.

"You said we have to get to Alora, so that's what we're doing," I explained. "You stay here and help Matt calm Sam down." I could see that Alex wanted to object again as I looked past her and Jules toward the spiral staircase that led to the fifth floor of the fun house. "Can Marie help us out without your being the one to go in with me?"

"What?" Jules looked around in confusion.

Alex looked behind her at the fun house and eventually nodded. "She said she'll lead you guys. I don't have time to explain, Jules, but Marie is here. She told me Alora was in trouble. You've *got* to get her out of there."

"Don't worry. We will," Jules promised.

Her gaze frantically went back and forth to the both of us. "*Please* be careful, and hurry," she said as her voice cracked from holding in a sob.

Without wasting any more time, we made our way to the spiral staircase. Jules led the way. The fair workers were so focused on controlling the growing crowd that they didn't notice us. Matt and Sam didn't notice what we were doing either until we were halfway up the stairs.

"Get back here!" Matt shouted. "You're going to get yourselves killed!"

We looked back for a split second and saw that all eyes were now on us. The crowd began screaming frantically. We could see mothers covering the eyes of their small children and looking away themselves. Smoke blew into our faces as we pressed on to the fifth floor.

"Marie?" Jules said in bewilderment when we looked to the top of the staircase. "Marie, wait! Slow down!" he shouted as he bolted to the fifth floor.

I looked toward where he was running but couldn't see anyone besides Jules.

—Chapter 25—

When we got to the top of the staircase, I stopped Jules before we went any further. "Where's Alora?"

Jules looked down the walkway of the fifth floor and nodded. "Marie said she's on the third floor. That's where the fire started."

I slowly stepped on the floor panels to make sure they didn't shift under us. I was relieved to discover that either the fire stopped everything from working or that the workers in charge of that particular attraction had cut the power off. "Lead the way."

Jules ran to the end of the walkway and took his time down the stairs that led to the fourth floor. He stopped dead in his tracks before going any further. "Be careful. You can break your leg on these things."

I looked and saw that the floors were made to make you feel like you were in a bounce house. Nodding, I followed him across the unstable floors as we fought to keep our balance. Once we got to the end, we took the stairs down to the third floor. When we got there, we saw the fire ripping through the curtains and melting away the wires and extension cords that once provided power to the lights.

"Marie, which way?" Jules asked.

I still couldn't see her, but as long as Jules could, I knew we'd be okay.

"She said to go left, make a right, and then make another left—and to also watch out for the broken glass."

We both got down as low as we could under the smoke and tried to stay away from cracked mirrors. As we walked, I saw pieces of a melted cell phone on the floor. When we reached the area where the broken glass was, we saw a bit of blood smeared on them. *I hope this isn't from Alora*, I thought.

"Marie went ahead. This is the first left we need to take," Jules coughed.

"Don't talk unless you absolutely have to. It'll cause you to inhale more smoke," I suggested.

He gave me a thumbs-up as I followed closely behind him. We soon came upon another split in the hallway, so we hung a right. The farther we went into the maze, the harder it was getting to breathe. Jules stopped abruptly when we heard someone faintly in the distance.

"Help! There are people trapped in here!"

Alora . . .

Our attention was directed to a loud creaking that came from the ceiling above us. We watched as some of it fell straight down. It must have landed on someone because we heard them scream in pain.

Jules motioned for us to continue. We quickened our pace as we got lower to the ground than we had been when we first entered the maze. Movement from ahead of us caught my attention through the smoke. I watched as Marie's reflection appeared in all of the mirrors that led up to the last hallway before the exit. She was holding a small red fire truck and was looking away from us.

"We need help!" I heard Alora gasp.

Marie continued to stare and didn't move a muscle. When we got up to her, Jules quickly hugged and thanked her for her help. I was in a state of shock. Marie then walked up to me and hugged me as well. The tighter she squeezed me, the more I felt my lungs filling with fresh oxygen. When she let go, I gazed at her as she started to fade away right before my eyes.

Jules got to his feet without struggling for breath. "I can see her!"

We ran up to Alora and another person who was lying on his back close to her. Everything around me started to clear as though I was inside the safety of a bubble. I could hear Alora coughing as we walked around the rubble that had fallen from the ceiling above us. I immediately recognized Jordan as his screams seemed to get louder and louder.

"Alora!" Jules stooped over and touched her shoulders. She went into another coughing fit as Jules scooped her up with little to no strain. "It's okay, Alora. I've got you. Everything will be okay."

"The guy trapped under the rubble is Jordan," I told Jules as I watched him get to his feet. "I have to get him out of here. You help Alora. I'll be right behind you."

"Be careful."

Glass began to shatter around us as he carried Alora toward the exit. I watched as he stumbled out of the door. Once I knew they had gotten out okay, I worked to figure out how to free Jordan's leg from under the rubble. His screaming was a huge distraction. "Shut up!" I shouted over the now roaring flames that were closing in on us. "At this rate, you'll pass out and get us both killed!"

Jordan closed his eyes and shut his mouth. He held his right thigh tightly as he tried to keep himself from screaming again. I found a piece of curtain that wasn't completely burned from the fire, ripped it in half, wrapped it around my hands, and flipped the obstruction off of his leg. There was no doubt that it was broken, but if I could get him out in time, that'd be the worst of his worries.

I kneeled down to him and grabbed both sides of his face. "Look at me!"

He opened his eyes and tried to focus on me as he started coughing.

"I'm going to get you out of here. Wrap your arms around my shoulders and hang on. Your leg is going to hurt, but I need you to hang in there until I can get us outside. Do you understand?"

He nodded exhaustedly as I grabbed his arms to sit him up. His face twisted from the pain as I positioned him so that I could get him onto my back. When I got his arms around my shoulders, he did everything in his power to help me get to my feet with his good leg. I held his wrists as I got him situated as if I were wearing a heavy backpack and slowly made my way to the exit.

Just as we started walking, a large piece of rubble fell and blocked our way out. I looked around in a panic as I tried to figure out where to go.

"Emergency . . . exit," Jordan rasped, "through . . . panels."

He moved his right elbow to show me which way to go. Without hesitation, I kicked the mirror in front of us, and it shattered into thousands of pieces. Feet away, I saw an emergency exit that led to the back of the fun house. I carried him as quickly as I could for fear that the emergency exit would end up getting blocked as well. When we got to the door, I pressed on the handle, and we were outside on metal rafters three floors from the ground. I could hear fire trucks pulling up around the front.

"We're almost safe, Jordan. Just hang on."

I put all of my strength into carrying him down three flights of stairs. Once we got to the bottom, we were intercepted by a group of firemen who were coming around the back to fight the fire from there. They dropped the hose they were about to turn on and ran up to us. "We didn't think you two were going to make it out alive," one of them said as they sat Jordan on the ground to take a look at his broken leg. "Quick! Get a stretcher for this guy," one of them ordered.

I stood back and watched as they checked over Jordan to make sure he wasn't severely burned or injured anywhere else. "Where's Alora? Is she okay?" I rasped.

"Who?" one of the firefighters asked.

"Alora Pebbles. Is she okay?"

"She's doing just fine thanks to you and your friend. That was a crazy stunt you two pulled. You could have gotten yourselves killed."

A smile formed on my face when I heard the news. "She's okay," I said woozily.

"You okay, son?" The firefighter placed his hand on my shoulder after I stumbled backward unprovoked. Without warning, the supply of fresh oxygen that Marie had provided escaped from me, and I passed out.

—Chapter 26—

Moonlight beamed on my face through my bedroom window as I sat up slowly. I winced when my head began to pound like someone was beating on it with a baton. I opened my eyes and allowed them to adjust to the darkness around me. When I realized I was in my room, I let out a sigh of relief as I flopped back into the pile of downy soft pillows. "That was a horrible nightmare." Leaning over, I turned on the light that was sitting on the nearby nightstand so I could find the remote for my TV.

After grabbing the remote, I let my arm fall limply by my side. It felt like it weighed thirty pounds; that's how sluggish and tired I felt. I couldn't understand why my body was so sore, but I ignored it. I figured it was from the overactive dream I had had. I turned on the TV that sat on the other side of the room on top of my dresser. The screen hummed as a picture began to appear. The channel was tuned in to the local news station and was on mute.

As the picture became clearer, I noticed that they were covering a developing story about a near-fatal accident that had occurred at the town fair that we all had attended earlier that night. I slowly turned it up so I could hear the reporter. After a few presses of the volume button, I could hear him loud and clear:

"Catastrophe struck earlier this week here at the annual town fair that was held here at the fairgrounds. Fire tore through this once-prized fun house that you see in ruins behind me. Two college students, whose names have not yet been released, were trapped inside on the third floor in the maze of mirrors. They were saved by two fellow college students, Julian Reed and James Stone. The investigation is ongoing, but as of right now, the police, as well as the fire department, are labeling the blaze an unfortunate accident. There were no casualties. The fair was brought to an end earlier than expected this year because of the incident but will hopefully return next year with a newer, and safer, fun house for the town to enjoy."

My eyes widened as I watched the fire department pick through the rubble behind the reporter, working to figure out how the fire had started to begin with. *That wasn't a dream?* I thought. *It actually happened?* I started to remember suffocating from the billowing smoke that was engulfing me, and Jordan's screaming when a piece of the ceiling landed on his leg. I looked at the nightstand I had grabbed the remote from and saw a bottle of white pills, an empty glass, and a broken hospital bracelet. The remote slowly fell out of my left hand as I pulled my right hand from under the blankets. It was wrapped in a thick layer of gauze; I then remembered how I had burned it trying to get Jordan's leg free. A million additional questions began running through my head as I stared blankly at the TV. Without giving it a second thought, I emitted a bloodcurdling scream. I heard Raven start barking from the front room as she and what sounded like two people rushed to my room. Raven charged in, jumped onto the bed, and pressed her cold, wet nose against mine, which caused me to stop screaming.

"It's okay, Alora. You're safe." Matt grabbed the remote from the bed and turned the TV off. Sam sat beside me and placed Raven on the floor.

"What happened?" I asked frantically.

"It's a long story," Sam stated. "But you're okay with the exception of your hand. The burn isn't too bad. The doctor says it'll take some time to heal and there'll be permanent scarring, but it'll be as good as new soon. Good thing you're left handed, huh?" she tried to joke.

I stared at her, still working to put the pieces together. "That's still not telling me what happened," I said flatly.

Sam looked to Matt. Raven was sitting on the floor between them as she wagged her tail slowly. "I'll talk to her. You should take Raven for her walk. It's been a few hours since she's been out."

Matt grabbed the empty glass and left the room. "Heel, Raven."

Raven stared at me and waited for me to give her the okay. "Go on, sweetie," I whispered.

She slowly walked out into the hallway with Matt. He closed the door behind them so Sam could talk to me in private. "First of all, I'm sorry I left you behind in the fun house like that. I should have stayed with you the entire way through. You wouldn't have gotten caught up in that mess because we would have been out before the fire started."

"It's not your fault." I massaged my right hand and dropped it lazily onto my lap. "The reporter on the TV said the accident happened earlier this week. Weren't we just there a few hours ago?"

"You've been going in and out of sleep ever since we brought you home from the hospital, so you've lost track of time and everything," Sam explained.

I looked over at the nightstand again and saw the broken hospital bracelet that someone had cut off of me. "And the pills?"

"They're for the pain and to help you rest. This isn't the first time you've jumped out of your sleep screaming like you were being murdered."

"I see . . ."

"The doctor said you were *very* lucky, Alora. If you had been in there a few minutes longer with all of that smoke, you would have had some serious complications—or worse."

My memory started to slowly come back to me. The last thing I remembered was burning my hand on the rubble that I tried to get off of Jordan's leg, seeing a little girl wearing a white dress, and hearing someone telling me I was going to be okay. "Where's Jordan? Is he okay?"

"I think he's getting released from the hospital tomorrow. He's got a broken leg and some minor burns, but that's it. He also took in a lot of smoke, so he would have been in more trouble if he were in the fun house any longer, too."

"Did the little girl get out safely?" I inquired.

"Huh?"

I sank into the blankets as I started feeling drowsy. Everything started to get blurry as I fought to keep my eyes open. "The little girl in the white dress holding the red fire truck—did she get out okay?"

"No one said anything about there being a child in there with the two of you," Sam said in confusion.

"I planned on wringing your neck for leaving me behind, you know that?" I laughed.

"I know, I know. And again, I'm sorry I did that to you. I promise to never do that again unless you tell me it's all right. Deal?"

"Deal," I slurred.

"Go back to sleep. We can talk more about what happened tomorrow."

I slowly fell back into a deep sleep without objecting. I felt Sam fluff some of the pillows around me and then get up from my bed.

The next morning, after my parents had checked in on me and left, I sat at the dining room table with Matt as we waited for Sam to finish making breakfast. It smelled good, but it made me feel nauseated. Matt could see it written all over my face and gave me a sympathetic smile. "You've only been drinking juice and water and nibbling on crackers while taking your meds. It's time you ate some real food."

I nodded and exhaled deeply as Sam placed a plate of scrambled eggs paired with a piece of toast in front of me. She then came back and sat half a glass of orange juice down along with two pills.

"There's no rush," Sam said as she placed a fuller plate of food in front of Matt along with a glass of juice. "If you can eat at least half of that, that'll be good enough."

I picked up the fork and poked at the eggs as Sam took a seat at the table with her breakfast. We all sat in silence as we ate. I managed to eat half of the eggs and all of the toast. When I was finished, I took both pills and drank all of the juice. Matt grabbed my plate and empty glass and took them into the kitchen.

We all looked to the front door when Alex walked in. Raven greeted her with a few playful yelps as she jumped all over her. Alex scratched her between her ears and then walked over to the table. "It's good to see you're up and moving." She gave me a light hug and had a seat next to me.

"I'm still a bit fuzzy about what happened," I admitted. "No one seems to know anything about the little girl I saw in the fun house."

Alex stared at me with a raised brow. "Little girl?"

"She's been going on about a little girl in a white dress since last night," Sam reminded her as she took her plate to the kitchen. "I keep trying to tell her that there wasn't anyone else in there except her and Jordan."

"Can you two go and check on the guys? Take Raven with you if it's not too much of a hassle."

Both Matt and Sam nodded. After they leashed Raven and left, we talked about what happened. "What do you remember from that night?" Alex asked.

"I remember—I remember that I got lost trying to find Sam in the mirror maze. And when I tried to go back to start from the beginning, I ran into Jordan and his friends. He took my phone and smashed it into pieces. I slapped and shoved him. Then I ran, and he ended up tripping on an extension cord and fell head first into one of the mirrors. The fire started soon after he tripped, but I didn't want to leave him there to die, so . . . I dragged him as far as I could until I couldn't drag him anymore. A piece of the ceiling fell on his leg, and I burned my hand trying to get it off of him." I touched my hand as I tried to remember what I had said the night before to Sam when we talked. It was throbbing so much that I was sure Alex could see it through the gauze.

"Take your time, Alora." Alex smiled softly. "If it's becoming too much, you can stop."

"After I burned my hand, I *saw* someone, Alexia. I saw a little girl. She stood there and stared even though I told her we needed help. Then I started coughing . . . and just as I started to black out, I felt like I was floating. I heard someone tell me that everything was going to be okay—and we headed toward a bright light."

Alex hung on to every word. "And then?"

"And then I woke up in my bed and turned on the TV to see the news coverage on the fire."

"I think the little girl you saw was a figment of your imagination because of all the smoke and fumes you inhaled," she said, trying to convince me. "Lack of oxygen can do that to you. There was no one else in there, like Matt and Sam told you. Well, except for James and Jules—"

"James? Where is he? Is he okay?" I asked frantically. I didn't give her time to answer; I could feel myself getting light-headed as I tried to suppress an anxiety attack. "Alex, *where's* James?" I looked at her in dismay, afraid of what she was going to tell me.

"Calm down, Alora. Breathe." Alex grabbed my right hand and gave it a gentle squeeze. "The person you heard telling you that everything would be okay? That was Jules. Both he and James went in to get you when we realized there was a fire and you hadn't rejoined us. James stayed behind to get Jordan out while Jules carried you to safety."

"But James *is* okay, right?"

"He's fine. They're both just exhausted. And I'm sure Matt or Sam told you that Jordan has a broken leg and some minor burns, but other than that, he's okay, too." Alex helped me out of my chair and walked me back to my room to lie down. "I wanted to go in after you at first, but James insisted that Jules go in my place. I wasn't too happy about it, but looking back, that was the right thing to do. I don't think I would have been able to carry you outside since you were unconscious."

She pulled back the blankets for me, and I slipped under them slowly as I worked to get comfortable. "I'll never be able to repay them for what they did for me."

"You making it out alive with only a burned hand is all the repayment they need." Alex closed the blinds so the sun wasn't pouring in. I could feel my eyes growing heavy as she sat on the bed next to me.

"Can you stay here until I'm asleep?" I asked sluggishly.

"Sure."

I tried to stay awake as I listened to Alex talk about how everyone was calling James and Jules heroes. I looked at the *Pick-up Stix* drawing that James had given me and smiled as I finally allowed my eyes to close and let the medication take over.

—Chapter 27—

"Catastrophe struck earlier this week here at the annual town fair that was held here at the fairgrounds. Fire tore through this once-prized fun house that you see in ruins behind me. Two college students, whose names have not yet been released, were trapped inside on the third floor in the maze of mirrors. They were saved by two fellow college students, Julian Reed and James Stone. The investigation is ongoing, but as of right now, the police, as well as the fire department, are labeling the blaze an unfortunate accident. There were no casualties. The fair was brought to an end earlier than expected this year because of the incident but will hopefully return next year with a newer, and safer, fun house for the town to enjoy."

"*Accident*," I mumbled as I shut the TV off and started to cough.

"You and I both know that Jordan didn't start the fire on purpose, James." Jules's voice was still raspy from inhaling so much smoke from the fire. "He tripped and fell, and it caused some lights to come crashing down. *That's* what started the fire. It's not like he went in there shooting fireballs all over the place like some crazy anime character."

"He wouldn't have tripped and fallen if he hadn't been going after Alora for slapping the mess out of him—which he deserved after what he admitted to doing to her when they were in there."

"I'm not saying he didn't deserve it. But *anyone* could have tripped on that cord at any time."

"I hate when you try to make me see both sides to everything." I sank deeper into the couch and closed my eyes.

Alex brought me a tall glass of water and then went and sat next to Jules. She handed him a glass of water as well. "I just got off of the phone with Sam. She said that Alora woke up screaming bloody murder again."

"Has she said anything about what happened?" I asked.

"She said something about seeing a little girl, who I'm assuming was Marie. How is that even possible?"

"I mean, did she say she saw *Marie*, or did she say she saw a little girl in a white dress?" Jules took a sip of water and began crunching on some of the ice cubes.

"She didn't say her name, just that she saw a little girl in a white dress holding a red fire truck. She wanted to know if she got out safely."

"I'm sure we can convince her that she was just hallucinating from a lack of oxygen or something." I held out my empty glass when I finished drinking the water. Alex reached over and took it from me. "And I'm sure that whatever reason Marie had to make herself visible to someone other than the three of us, it was a good one. How's her hand? Is it okay?"

"They said she noticed it was bandaged for the first time when she woke up tonight but didn't say much about it since she ended up falling back to sleep after telling Sam how she had planned to wring her neck that night."

The three of us laughed quietly. We all were imagining how that'd look if it actually happened.

"Strangely enough, since this whole incident happened, I've been sleeping better," Alex said guiltily. "You'd think I'd be up worried about the three of you."

"I'm just glad your nightmares and headaches went away. Maybe what you were dreaming about had to do with what happened. It'll take some time to figure out what your gift is. Until then, we'll just take it one day at a time," Jules coughed.

"It was crazy how Marie came to the three of us, though. I admit, at first I couldn't see her and I thought Alex was delusional from lack of sleep. But when you said you could see her, Jules, that's when I had a moment of clarity. Things became very real for me when she appeared to me in that last hallway and she gave us that extra air we'd need to get everyone out."

Both Alex and Jules nodded in agreement.

"The loss of that fresh air when I got out of there was the kicker," Jules chuckled. "Seconds after a firefighter took Alora out of my arms, I passed out."

"Same thing happened to me when I found out she was okay and they started looking over Jordan," I admitted.

"I wonder if he realizes he's forever in your debt because you saved his life," Alex pointed out.

I snickered at the thought. "Knowing him, he'll brush it off and not give it a second thought."

The next morning, Jules and I watched sports highlights while falling in and out of sleep. Unlike Alora, we hadn't been prescribed medication. We were just exhausted from what happened and got some decent shut-eye when we could. Light knocking at the front door prompted Jules to get up and answer it. I had been staying at his place ever since the incident. Matt and Sam walked in with Raven. She ran around the couch and jumped on me happily. "Hey, there." I wrestled her with my hands for a moment, and then I unclipped the leash from her collar and sat her back down on the floor. "What's going on, guys?"

"Alora's parents left a while ago. They came by to check on her; now Alex is over there talking to her," Sam said as she got comfortable in the loveseat across from us. Matt stood next to her. "She brought up that little girl she thinks she saw in the fun house again, so Alex asked us to come over to check on you guys. I'm sure she can help her make sense of everything. Did *you* two see anyone other than Alora and Jordan when you went in after her?"

We both shook our heads simultaneously. "I'm sure she was just seeing things," Jules answered.

A knock at the door caused Raven to run to it and start barking. We all stared at one another and didn't say anything until there was another quiet knock.

"You guys expecting company?" Sam asked suspiciously.

I shrugged. "Not that I know of."

Matt left Sam's side and answered the door. Raven stuck her head out into the breezeway and started wagging her tail.

"Mind if we come in?" I heard an older gentleman ask.

"Uh—sure."

Matt moved to the side and opened the door wider. Jules's and Sam's eyes widened as Raven continued to bark excitedly. Matt picked her up and took her into Jules's bathroom. Once he locked her in there, she instantly fell silent. He then went over and stood by Sam again. She slowly got to her feet, and so did Jules. I was still facing the TV.

"Well, who is it?"

I turned on the couch and saw Jordan standing in the doorway with his parents on either side of him. He was struggling with his crutches as he tried to keep his balance. His right leg from his foot up to his knee was in a cast, and he had stitches on his forehead. I immediately got to my feet like Jules and Sam.

"I hope we aren't interrupting anything," Jordan's mother said quietly.

Jules shook his head. "No, not at all."

"Mind if Jordan has a seat?" his father asked. "He's got a few things he'd like to say to both you and James."

"Please," Jules said.

Jordan took a seat at the dining room table while his parents stood behind him. Matt and Sam sat in the front room on the couch I had been sitting on while Jules sat at the end of the table, and I sat across from Jordan.

"First and foremost, *we* want to thank you for saving our son's life. We know how risky it was for you to stay behind to make sure he got out safely after Julian got Alora out of the fire," Jordan's father said quietly.

"To be honest, Alora did most of the work," I told them. "He may not have made it if she hadn't gotten him as close to the exit as she possibly could."

"We'll make sure we speak to her personally sometime today. We know she has some recuperating to do with her hand and everything," Jordan's mother said.

"We're sure she'll bounce back within the next week or so. Either way, she'll be fine by the time the fall semester starts. She'll be home until then, but we can't guarantee she'll be awake when you stop by. It wouldn't hurt to try, though," Jules informed them.

"Good thing she's left handed, huh?" Jordan blurted out.

His father slapped him in the back of the head. "We brought you here so you could do the right thing, Jordan, not make jokes," his father reminded him.

I could see on Jordan's face how embarrassed he was that that just happened in front of everyone. He eyed both of us and then looked down at the table with a sigh. "I came here today to apologize for everything. And when I say everything, I mean *everything*. Julian, I know I've been giving you a hard time ever since you moved here almost two years ago. I don't know why I do some of the things I do, to be honest. Maybe I'm insecure or just overly confident . . . or I let what I have, and what I'm capable of doing or getting, go to my head. It's no excuse, though. I'll have a lot of time to work on myself with this broken leg and all."

Jules nodded to show that he accepted his apology.

"And James . . ."

He looked me straight in the eye, and I matched his gaze. He dug into his shorts pocket and slid a check across the table to me. It was the one I had written out to him to buy Alora's furniture and to replenish whatever gas he had used to come by that day. "You were right. It was a waste of a trip to drive all the way over here to take something from Alora that she needed more than me. I wasn't happy to see that she had moved on as quickly as she did. I was going out of my way to make sure she was miserable, so seeing her happy with you and her friends rubbed me the wrong way. I'm extremely grateful that you got me out of the fire in one piece. I have a broken leg, but things could have been much worse." He dug into his pocket again and pulled out a cell phone, which he also slid across the table to me. "If no one told you already, I smashed Alora's phone that night before the fire started. This one was mine; I bought it earlier that day. I cleared out all of my contacts, put the phone in her name, and made sure her original number was transferred to it. If you could give it to her so she has something to get in touch with her parents so they don't have to drive out here to check on her and so that she can call you guys, I'd appreciate it."

I took the phone and turned it on. Just as he had said, it was wiped clean of anything he had on it when he was using it. "Any particular reason as to why *you* won't give it to her?"

"I'm sure she won't take anything from me anymore after all that crap I said about her always accepting handouts and all. I wouldn't blame her."

I nodded and placed the phone on top of the check.

"I owe you my life," he said as he got a little teary eyed. "And I feel horrible for the way I've been to Alora, and Julian, and Alexia. Karma sure did do a number on me. If there's anything you need from me, anything at all, I'll make it happen, I swear. I'm forever in your debt."

I looked at Jules, and he nodded to me. I knew that he was thinking the same thing I was thinking, so I didn't hesitate to make a request right then and there.

"Get over Alora. I know that sounds really harsh with everything that's happened recently, but you *really* hurt her. And every time you pop up, it doesn't just stress her out; it stresses *all* of us out. I'd rather not have you anywhere near her, or us, until you know how to conduct yourself without being so offensive or toxic. I've taken your place, and Alora has been happier ever since. Understand?"

Jordan nodded.

"Also, I don't know what the deal is with you and your constant need to push Jules around, but that needs to end *today*. I know you said you don't know why you do some of the things you do, and you gave a few possible reasons, but you need to stop making excuses. You and Alex don't get along because of the way you've treated Alora all these years, which drove them apart for a while. Bottom line, don't forget to think of all the people you've negatively affected while you work on yourself," I ended.

"I understand," Jordan stammered.

"Did you have anything else to say, son?" his father asked.

"No, sir."

"Let's get you home then. The police will be over later to talk to you about the cause of the fire. We'll bring you back over here later so you can talk to Alora and Alexia."

"Yes, sir."

Jules got up and opened the front door for the three of them. Jordan's father led the way out, and his mother followed closely behind Jordan. Once Jules saw them get to the first floor without any issues, Jules quietly closed the door and locked it. Matt went to let Raven out of the bathroom. She bolted out expecting to see Jordan but was disappointed when she discovered that he was no longer there.

"How random was that?" Sam said as she came over to us from the couch.

"Do you really think he'll get his act together, though?" Matt asked, sounding skeptical.

"If his parents have anything to do with it, he will." Jules sat down at the dining room table again and slouched in the chair.

"We should probably head back over to Alex and Alora's place to check up on her." Sam grabbed Raven's leash and clipped it to her collar.

"Okay. Jules, I'm actually going to head up to my apartment now before I overstay my welcome." I scooped Alora's new phone and my check from the table.

"Are you sure?" Jules said with a raised brow.

"Yeah. I'll come by later so we can go over to visit Alora. I have something to do before we go over there."

"Okay. See you guys later, then."

I waved to Matt and Sam as they walked Raven back over to Alex and Alora's apartment. I slowly walked to the third floor and entered mine. Everything was still where I had left it the night I had wrapped the *Pick-up Stix* drawing for Alora. After taking a quick shower, I sat at the dining room table and began putting the finishing touches on what I knew would make Alora smile from ear to ear when we went to check on her later that day.

—Chapter 28—

When Alex answered the door a few minutes after Matt and Sam had left for the day, she found the three of them standing there—Jordan and his parents—and was at a loss for words. I was sleeping when she came in and woke me up to tell me that they were sitting at the dining room table.

"I thought you said he has a broken leg," I said as I swung my legs over the side of the bed and slipped on a pair of slippers.

"He does." Alex sat next to me and lowered her voice to a whisper. "His parents must have helped him up *all* three flights of stairs. That can't be good for his leg, but

I'm sure there's a reason behind why they made him go to great lengths to speak with us."

"That's quite the punishment."

"I can tell them you're asleep if you don't want to deal with him right now." Alex helped me get to my feet.

"He came up three flights of stairs to meet with me when he could be at home drugged up and sleeping. I'm not going to turn him away after he struggled to get up here. Plus, I'd rather get whatever this is out of the way now so I won't have to deal with it later."

Once we were seated across from him, we waited for him to speak. He looked as though he was trying to think of the words to say. I was growing impatient because I wanted to go back to bed.

"First and foremost, *we* want to thank you for saving our son's life. We know how risky it was for you to get him as close to the exit as you possibly could. You could have saved yourself, but you went back for him," Jordan's father said quietly.

"To be honest, James was the one who did the most important part of saving his life," I told them. "He may not have made it if James hadn't freed his leg and carried him out of the emergency exit."

Jordan's father smiled and shook his head. "You and James are very humble. Neither of you are willing to take all of the credit for getting him out of there safely. That's very noble of the both of you."

"You spoke to James?" Alex cut in.

"We came over to this side of town earlier today so Jordan could talk to both James and Julian. We brought him back so he could speak to the both of you. Go on, son. We don't want to hold them up," Jordan's mother pressed.

"Alexia, I want to apologize for giving you a hard time the way I've been. Alora is lucky to have a friend like you who doesn't let her go up against someone or something alone. The guys who I *thought* were my friends ditched me in the fun house and left me to die. If it were you two in that situation, I know you would have stuck together. And I'm *extremely* sorry for causing you to hurt yourself at the diner that one day. I can only imagine what it felt like hitting your leg as hard as you did. It was really immature of me . . . I should have left you both alone to have your lunch and gone about my business."

I looked over at Alex. She flashed a smile and gave a light nod. "I accept your apology," she said as she reached across the table and took his hand. "I can tell you're being sincere. I have a business card for the physical therapist I was seeing for my leg if you'd like it. They'll work around your schedule, and they won't push you too hard."

"We'd like that very much, Alexia. Thank you," Jordan's father said.

"I'm not too sure what to say to you, Alora," Jordan began.

My stomach sank when he said that, but I let him continue without interrupting him.

"I know I changed, and things went downhill with the two of us. None of it was your fault, and I'm sorry I blindsided you with the whole breakup bit. I deserved that slap in the face when you ran into us in the mirror maze; you were right, what I did was uncalled for. Like my father said, you could have left me for dead when you saw my friends leave and I wasn't with them. You were *right* there staring the exit in the face . . . but you came back for me. I'll be forever grateful for that. I swear to you, I won't get in your way anymore. If I see you in passing and you see me, I'll be respectful to you and the people you're with. I've already gone over this with James and Julian, so I'm sure they'll fill you in on the details. All I ask is that you forgive me for everything that I've ever done to you."

"That'll take some time," I said flatly without hesitation. "I know you're here with the best intentions, but I can't sit here and magically erase everything you've put me through from my memory. I can only imagine what would've happened to me in that fun house if it were the other way around and I had been the one who had gone head first into a mirror. I know for a *fact* that you wouldn't have come back for me."

"C'mon, Alora. Don't act like you didn't consider leaving me behind," he countered.

"Of course I did. And I'm not ashamed to admit it. You have *no* idea what kind of effect you have on people. For a split second, I told myself that if you were hurt, it was your own fault. But I couldn't do that to you, no matter what you've done to me."

"And again, I'm glad you came back for me—"

"I'll believe you when I see changes in you as a person. You'll have plenty of time with that broken leg of yours to reflect on everything you've done to *any* of us. Karma is a bitch, isn't it?"

"Apparently," he sighed.

"Your apology has been duly noted." I got to my feet and pushed the chair back under the table. "I need to rest. I've been on medication ever since I left the hospital, and I need to start sleeping it all off so I can be a functioning member of society before I can go back to work and before the fall semester starts. I'll see you around."

I excused myself and slowly walked back to my room without Alex's help. She stayed out front to talk to Jordan's parents about the physical therapist in depth. I curled up in my bed and sank into the pillows as I drifted back to sleep as if the meeting that had just occurred hadn't happened.

—Chapter 29—

Alex woke Alora up when we got there later on in the evening. We waited for her in the front room as she freshened up. Alex sat down with Jules on the loveseat, and I patiently waited for Alora on the couch. Raven was stretched out by the front door, nodding. When Alora came out and approached me, I got up and gave her a bear hug. "How's your hand?"

"It hurts, but I'll live." We both sat down and got comfortable. "How're you guys?" she asked.

"We're just tired," Jules told her. "The entire ordeal took a lot out of us."

"I can't thank you two enough for coming in to get me. You didn't even know that Jordan was in there with me, but you got him out safely too. With the way he's treated you guys, I would have half-expected you to leave him behind."

"Yeah, well, we talked about that earlier today," I said. "Jordan said he's in our debt and that we'll see a different side of him because of that. But until I see the changes for myself, I don't want him anywhere near us."

"I agree," Jules concurred.

"I don't know. I thought his apology seemed pretty genuine," Alex said thoughtfully.

"I figured *you* of all people wouldn't trust his word," Alora argued. "I was a bit shocked when you accepted his apology with no reservation."

"There was something about it that was very sincere. I really don't think we'll have any more trouble from him."

"I guess we'll find out once classes are back in session," Jules said with a shrug.

I dug into my pocket and gave Alora the cell phone that Jordan had given me. "I don't know if he apologized to you for what he did to your phone, but he told me to give this to you. He said it's in your name, and your phone number was transferred over to it."

"Oh?" She turned it on and went to the contacts list. She quickly added all of our numbers into it. "He didn't have to do that. I would have gotten a replacement phone on my own at some point."

"You know what else he didn't have to do?"

I pulled the check out of my pocket and showed it to her as well. When Alex and Jules asked for the backstory, we told them what had happened the day we were moving Alex and Alora into their place.

"I can't believe you gave him what he wanted," Jules said, shaking his head.

"She needed the furniture. If he had taken it back, she'd have nothing, and you guys would have a half-furnished apartment. It's not like I didn't have the money to spare." I folded the check and placed it back in my pocket for safekeeping until I could destroy it properly.

"Still," Alex said, taking Jules's side, "you should have come and gotten us. He would have left since he would have been outnumbered. The furniture wouldn't have gone anywhere."

"What matters is that the check wasn't cashed, and we still have the furniture. I'd say it's a win-win situation." Alora sat up when she saw a wrapped box sitting on the coffee table across from us. "What's that?"

"It's a get-well-soon gift." I reached over and grabbed it for her. She took it from me and inspected the wrapping paper. "I know the wrap job isn't all that great, but I figured I'd give it a shot anyway."

"I don't care about that." She smiled as she started to open it.

The only sound in the apartment for a few moments was that of wrapping paper being ripped and balled up. I had wrapped the gift in a few layers so that she had to work to get to the center of it. Raven woke up when she first heard the sound and got up on the couch to watch as well. She took the bow when she thought no one was looking and ran off with it.

When Alora finally got to the center of the wrapping paper, she held her semi-new keepsake box up in the light. After replacing the damaged lid with a new one, and connecting it to the original base, I engraved the same picture from the drawing hanging in her room into the lid. I bought special paint to fill in what were supposed to be the sticks.

"This is better than the original," she gasped.

"That means you like it, then?"

"I absolutely *love* it."

I opened it for her, and inside was the small stuffed giraffe from our night at the town fair. "I didn't necessarily win this for you. The booth operator only gave it to me because I was being a good sport."

"He really sucks at games, especially the rigged ones," Jules laughed.

"I hit those bottles dead on!" I shot back as I chucked a throw pillow at him.

"I don't care how you got it. I think he's cute." Alora took the toy out of the box, stroked the giraffe's fur between its ears, and played with the hair at the tip of its tail. "What did you win for Alex, Jules?"

"An oversized stuffed dog, and Matt won Sam a large bean-stuffed snake," he answered proudly. "I'm actually surprised that they were still at the table where we left them. Anyone could have taken off with them. Someone was kind enough to put them somewhere safe."

Alora placed the giraffe back into the box when she noticed that Raven had ditched the bow she had taken and was eyeing the giraffe. "This isn't for you." She then pointed at the bow. Raven grabbed it and brought it to her. "*This* isn't for you, either." After she took it, she gave Raven a playful bop on the head.

Jules and I filled Alex and Alora in on what Jordan had said to us earlier that morning. They listened without interruption until we were finished.

"I still don't want anything to do with him until I see some kind of change," I reiterated. "I get stressed out by just hearing his name."

"I think this incident was a real eye-opener for him. I seriously do think he'll change for the better. He may have a couple of setbacks here and there, but that's to be expected. It happens to everyone." Alex got up and stretched; Jules did the same.

"Maybe." Alora yawned at the same time as Raven, who was sitting in her lap comfortably. "Like Jules said, we'll find out when classes are back in session."

Before we left their place, I walked Alora to her room to wish her a good night. I placed her new keepsake box on her dresser and waited until she was settled in bed. I looked at the broken hospital bracelet on her nightstand and the bottle of medication that was sitting close by.

"I hate taking those things," she said when she noticed me looking at them. "I wish I had it easy like you and Jules and not have to take anything." She held up her right hand that was wrapped in fresh gauze.

"It's not as easy as we make it out to be."

"Before you go, I have to ask you something."

"Shoot."

"Did you see a little girl in a white dress in the fun house when you two came in to get me?" she asked as she lay on her side and got comfortable.

I sat on the bed next to her. "Alora, you and Jordan were the *only* two people in there when the fire started. Then there were four of us total when we came in. There was *no* little girl. You really need to let that go, okay? People are going to start thinking you're crazy if you keep talking about a person who doesn't exist."

She sighed in defeat. "Okay . . . but only because *you* insist."

"Do you need anything for any of your classes? I can grab whatever it is when I get the chance."

"I've already gotten everything, but thank you."

I waited until she was sound asleep before I left her room and closed the door behind me. Alex and Jules were waiting in the front room. "She brought up Marie again," I whispered. "But I think I've convinced her to finally let it go."

"Okay, good." Alex sounded relieved. "I was getting tired of using the same explanation as to why she thinks she saw someone else in the fire. I was starting to feel like a broken record."

We said good-night to Alex and made our way home. We took our time since there was no rush to get back. As we walked, we looked up into the clear night sky; the moon was full, and we could see all the stars.

"You did an amazing job with that keepsake box, James." Jules patted me on the shoulder. "I knew you'd pull it off regardless of what you did, but you definitely went above and beyond. And you know what else? You actually met your personal deadline. You didn't realize that, did you?" he pointed out.

I remembered how I had said I wanted to win Alora over before the fall semester started. From the way things were going at first, that didn't seem obtainable. Now it felt as though the huge bump in the road that had been there in the beginning was never there to start with. "No, I didn't realize that until you brought it up."

"I'm proud of you for hanging in there."

"Without the help of you and Alex, it may not have been possible."

"We just helped you stay focused and gave you two a gentle push in the right direction. In the end, this all came to fruition because of the steps *you* took to obtain your original goal. I'm sure G is proud."

As we approached our building, I noticed a star begin to shine brighter than all the others for a moment and then grow dim to blend back in.

"I don't doubt it," I said with a smirk.

—Chapter 30—

"*La prueba del viernes cubrirá las palabras del vocabulario que le di la semana pasada. Veré a todos ustedes entonces. ¡Disfrute del resto de su día!*"

The four of us walked out of our elementary Spanish class and headed toward the courtyard. James grabbed my right hand and gave it a gentle squeeze on the way outside. I didn't have to wear gauze around it anymore because it was healing nicely. There'd always be a scar, but it was something I didn't mind having since it reminded me of my selfless act.

"So what'd the professor say is happening on Friday?" Jules asked Alex as they led the way.

She gave him a playful shove. "You don't pay very much attention when it comes to this class, do you?"

"How can I when you're a huge distraction the entire time?"

"You're the cheesiest person I know, you know that?"

"You love it." He wrapped his arm around her shoulders as we got closer to the table where Matt and Sam were sitting. They waved us down when they saw us, so we headed toward them.

"There's going to be a test on Friday about the feminine and masculine tenses for some of the vocab words she gave us last week. It should be fairly easy if it's multiple choice," I answered. "We should probably study sometime tonight or tomorrow. I made some flash cards for everyone, so we should be fine. Or maybe even Matt and Sam could quiz the four of us together during our break between classes today so we can get a head start."

"Well, we work late tonight, so unless these two are okay with waiting up for us, we should probably shoot for now or put it off until tomorrow since we'll be off then." Alex sat her things on the table after Matt and Sam moved their books to the side. Jules sat next to her and bumped her shoulder with his and smiled.

"Either day works for me." James took a seat and placed his bag on the ground close by.

I was about to have a seat next to him when I heard laughter coming from the other side of the courtyard. I looked around and saw Jordan struggling with his backpack. Some of his things were falling out of it onto the ground, and he was having a hard time picking everything back up with his crutches being in the way.

"He probably should have signed up for online classes. I'm sure his counselor would have made the last-minute change for him because of his situation." Sam said empathetically.

"I kind of feel sorry for him," Matt said solemnly.

I looked to James, and it was obvious that he knew what I was thinking. He gave me a nod, and I made my way over to Jordan to help him before he hurt himself. As I got closer to him, I heard him cursing under his breath. Every time he tried to put his things back into his bag, other items would fall out. I got there just in time; one of the crutches was coming out from under his arm, and he didn't notice. I grabbed it just before it fell to the ground. He looked at me in shock and then looked away in embarrassment. "Someone unzipped my bag during class to give me a hard time."

"I can see that." I took his bag out of his hand so he could get himself together on his crutches. "You should probably check your things at the end of all your classes to make sure no one tampered with your stuff. You could be here all day if this happens again."

"How could no one stop to help me? I *know* they see I'm on crutches."

"Well, how could you *not* move out of Jules's way the first day we met him and you purposefully bumped into him? You made him pick up all of *your* books and still got nasty with him when he apologized for something that wasn't his fault, remember?" I carefully put everything back inside his bag and zipped it closed.

"Thank you for helping me." He gave a nervous wave to the table everyone was sitting at. They waved back.

"Did you need help to your next class?" I asked as I put his bag on my back.

"If it won't get you into trouble or anything, I'd appreciate it."

"In trouble?"

"You know, with James."

I laughed and gestured for him to start walking. "You're the *only* one who got angry about stupid stuff like that." I waved to the table to get James's attention. He saw that I was walking with Jordan and waved back. "I just let him know where I'm going or what I'm doing out of respect."

"I guess that's where I messed up with you, huh?"

"You messed up in a lot of departments, Jordan. But you're working on it, right?"

"Right."

I helped him get seated in his psychology class and sat with him for a few minutes to keep him company. He told me that the doctors were hopeful that he'd be out of the cast by the time winter break arrived. "I plan on going to the physical therapist that Alexia referred me to. Can you tell her I said thank you again?"

"Sure." I got up and pushed his bag closer to him so no one would mess with it when he wasn't looking. "I should get going."

"Thank you for sitting with me for a while before class started. No one has talked to me since the fire. I didn't start it purposefully, but the events that led up to it have a lot of people angry with me."

"Don't mention it. Make sure you check your bag after all of your classes. Everyone will get over what happened eventually. Until then, look at it as karma still doing its handiwork until it's finished with you."

"There's no doubt in my mind that that's what's happening. It was good seeing you."

I left the classroom and headed back out to the courtyard. Everyone was still at the table with their textbooks and notepads open. I sat next to James and grabbed the Spanish flash cards out of my purse. "Would you guys mind quizzing us for our test on Friday? You can start with Jules since he's falling behind."

"Thanks for volunteering me," he said with a frown as he watched me pass the cards across the table to Matt and Sam. They split the stack in half so they each had different questions to ask.

"Okay, Jules, the word for *sneaker*, or *shoe*, is what?" Matt asked.

We all watched as Jules struggled with the answer. His facial expressions were priceless; if it was possible, we'd see steam coming out of his ears because he was thinking so hard. "I know this. Just give me another minute."

"Hey," James tapped me on my shoulder and cleared his throat. "*¿Todo bien?*" he asked.

"This guy," Jules teased. "He was so worried about taking a foreign language, but he speaks it as though it's his first language. I can't even remember the word for *shoe*."

"It's *zapato*, Jules," I giggled. "And yes, everything's okay—better than okay, if you ask me."

Before I went to work that evening, I asked James to come with me to the beach so we could sit and talk for a bit. It had been a while since we had gone there, so I thought it'd be the perfect spot to have a few minutes of alone time together.

"That was very big of you to help Jordan today." James shoved his bare feet into the sand and wiggled his toes. "I know that was difficult with everything he's put you through and all."

"He's been doing a really good job of holding up his end of the bargain. It'll take some time to put everything behind us, but as long as he keeps going the way he is, he'll be just another face on campus, one that I won't want to punch or anything."

"One can only hope."

"I asked you to come out here because I just wanted to tell you how much I appreciate everything you've done for me since we've met. Whether you know it or not, you've helped me in more ways than you can imagine."

He extended his hand, and I placed my right one into it. He gave it a gentle squeeze and smiled. "I guess we can say the universe did right by the both of us."

I smiled thoughtfully as I inhaled deeply through my nose to take in the smell of the ocean. "It most certainly did."

—Epilogue—

I took it upon myself to buy this notebook like James suggested the night we were all together at the fair. I'm hoping it'll help me, like going to the beach helped Alora.

So . . . here goes nothing:

I feel terrible.

I've been lying to both James and Jules about the nightmares. The only thing that stopped is the headaches, which my physical therapist said would go away eventually. I wish they would have stuck around and the nightmares would have gone away instead. I can at least take something for the headaches. I can't take a pill to chase away bad dreams.

What's even worse is that I didn't tell James everything about the nightmare the day he said he needed to talk to me. It's bad enough that I asked him to keep this from Jules; the last thing I need is for him to worry about me more than he already does. Then I also promised James I'd tell him if there were any changes in the nightmares—which I haven't been doing, either.

I feel like I'm creating a god-awful mess that I won't be able to fix when things hit the fan. And if Jules finds out that James has been lying to him, on top of my lying to him, too, I can only imagine how betrayed he'll feel.

The nightmares are getting more detailed, but they aren't detailed enough at the same time. It's driving me insane! The same dark figure has been appearing, but I can't make out who, or what, it is. Whatever it is, it's dangerous. And I feel like at some point, it'll manifest itself outside of the nightmares. What if they're signs that something bad is going to happen soon?

We're still trying to figure out my gift. That's not making me feel any better about any of this, either, so I feel useless. James and Jules are lucky; they have their gifts down pat. I don't know if I have a heightened sense of empathy or the ability to see dead people under the right circumstances. I wish I had gotten to talk to Marie that night at the fair. I haven't seen her since then. Maybe she could have told me about the nightmares. Ever since the fire, though, there have been times when I see bright colors hovering over people when I'm out. After a few seconds, sometimes even minutes, though, the colors disappear. It's weird; every time it happens, the colors are different. But then again, what's going on around me is different every time, too.

I don't know . . .

I'm not feeling any better about this by just writing it down. I'd much rather talk to someone. James swears he'd understand because we're one and the same. But he's taken what happened to him like a duck takes to water. I didn't ask for any *of what happened to me. I didn't want a hairline fracture in my leg or a pipe to go through it and my side . . . I didn't want to go through two years of physical therapy. And I* don't *want nightmares every other night.*

I'd better get going; I have to get to work. Maybe if I actually write when I wake up from one of the nightmares like James suggested, it'll help me piece together what's going on. So far, all I can remember are lush trees, cliffs, the dark figure, and the six of us together. If you take the dark figure out of the equation, it's actually the perfect dream I'd want to have—the six of us somewhere with that kind of scenery, you know? But when the dark figure shows up, that's when things go awry . . .

That's when I start fighting to wake up because I can sense that something, or someone, is trying to hurt one or all of us.

—*A.W.*